"From the moment I saw you, I decided that I wanted you."

Conrad's fingers moved through Jo's hair, curved down the back of her head and massaged her sensitive nape. "You don't even know me," she breathed.

"Survival out here is a question of cutting through the false veneer of civilization and discovering what lies below. I'm a simple man. Come out with me to the prairie, face adversity and find out who you really are."

Jo thought he was going to kiss her, and she stiffened in anticipation of his touch. "I know who I am."

"No...I don't think you do know," he said, his voice low. "You're a beautiful woman, Jo. Too bad you fight it so hard."

And with that, he was gone.

CLAIRE HARRISON

an independent woman

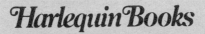

Harlequin Books

TORONTO • NEW YORK • LONDON
AMSTERDAM • PARIS • SYDNEY • HAMBURG
STOCKHOLM • ATHENS • TOKYO • MILAN

Harlequin Presents first edition January 1985
ISBN 0-373-10753-6

Original hardcover edition published in 1984
by Mills & Boon Limited

CHAPTER ONE

Jo DAVIDSON zipped her blue windbreaker up tighter to her neck and wrapped her arms tightly around her knees as she sat before the campfire. She wasn't the type to be nervous or uneasy in the dark, but this evening seemed to be an exception. She hadn't yet grown accustomed to the way nightfall came in the Canadian Rockies. It was as if a curtain had been pulled down across the sun, and she was still astonished that it could be light one minute and then virtually black the next. Churning clouds obscured the moon and stars, and only the tiny fire and the thin yellow beam of a kerosene lamp, hanging on a nearby tree, provided any illumination for her campsite. Above her head, the trees creaked and groaned as their branches yielded to the force of the wind, and Jo could feel her black shoulder-length hair whipping around her face.

An owl hooted in the distance, and the leaves underfoot crackled and snapped as if alive with small creatures. Even Jo who was apt to scoff at such things found it spooky. She shivered slightly in the chill of the night air and huddled closer to the fire. A cold front had come through the Rockies that afternoon, and Jo suspected that a midnight thunderstorm might be on the cards. She felt safe enough with her small, compact tent guy-wired securely to the ground, but she found herself longing for Emily's companionship and thinking that she'd give anything to have her sister sitting beside her rather than lying in a hospital bed.

Whenever she thought back on the morning's events, Jo found herself mentally repeating a tiresome refrain. *If only. If only* Emily had worn her cleated boots instead of those old sneakers with the treads worn off like used tires. *If only* she hadn't been in such a hurry that Emily had been obliged to run after her. *If only* Emily had been as sure-footed as a goat and not tumbled down the stairs outside that restaurant. *If only* Emily hadn't broken her ankle in three places, requiring a full-leg cast and complete bed rest for a week. *If only . . .*

Jo shook her head in sorrowful regret. What was the use of crying over spilt milk? The accident had happened, and she was left holding the shattered plans of their vacation plus all the problems of getting them back home. Emily's leg cast, she knew, would not fit in the front of her tiny car, and besides she doubted if her sister would be capable of the 2,500 mile trip home by car. That meant Emily had to go back by plane. Who would meet her? Who would get her home and up the narrow stairs to the small apartment the sisters shared in their hometown of Fairfax, New York? Who would cook, shop and clean for her while Jo drove the long trip back; easily a four-day trek?

A shower of sparks caused Jo to sit back slightly as she unhappily reassessed the situation for the thousandth time that day. Emily's broken ankle would be a real blow to their financial situation, especially if she had to be flown from Calgary to New York. Their trip to the Canadian West had eaten up most of their available resources, and Jo wasn't sure just how much their medical insurance would cover of Emily's expenses. She frowned as she estimated the extent of their meagre savings account, the value of the few stocks and bonds they held from their grandmother's estate and the depleted balance of their checking account. So tight was the money situation that Jo didn't feel she could afford to spend the night in a motel in the small Alberta town of Pincher Creek where the hospital was situated. Instead, she had decided to camp in Waterton National Park where she and Emily had stayed the night before.

So much for best-laid plans, she thought ruefully, cupping her chin in her hand and staring broodingly into the glowing embers of the fire. Well, she'd manage somehow; she knew that. She was accustomed to taking care of Emily. Despite the four year split in their ages; her twenty-six to Emily's twenty-two, Jo's feelings towards Emily were more motherly than sisterly. Their parents had divorced when Jo was five and Emily was one, and in the difficult years of adjustment that followed, she had taken a fierce and loving possession of her sister. It was Jo who had banished away Emily's fanciful nightmares and soothed cuts and hurts. It was Jo who had later helped Emily make the decision to become a kindergarten teacher. Their mother, Prudence, had been too unhappy and too busy trying to create a new life for herself to spend time with her daughters.

Even though they were both over twenty-one, Jo still found herself feeling responsible for her sister. It wasn't that Emily couldn't take care of herself; in fact, they were apartment-mates and equally shared responsibility for all household chores. Jo just felt that Emily was vulnerable. She worried too much about other people and trivial things. And she had a soft heart that Jo saw as hopelessly forgiving. Emily was the kind of person who would take a bedraggled stranger off the street and give him, metaphorically speaking, the shirt off her back. Jo, on the contrary, felt that she was made of tougher stuff. She was more cynical, more experienced about people. Emily had had Jo to protect her; Jo had had no one.

And just as if personality differences weren't enough, the sisters didn't resemble one another at all. Emily was short, blonde and slender with a small nose covered with freckles and big round blue eyes. Jo was tall and willowy, her complexion a smooth olive, her features cameo-pure, her eyes a striking shade of dark amber against the black of her hair, eyebrows and lashes. Nature had conspired to make them opposites, but the ties of love between them were stronger for the differences.

Which made Jo's feelings of guilt even stronger. She had the uncomfortable feeling that Emily's broken ankle was all her fault. Camping had never been one of Emily's favourite activities; Jo had always known that. If she'd given in to her sister's desire to visit a hotel in the Adirondacks, they'd have done nothing more strenuous than play tennis and choose evening clothes for dances after dinner. But she hadn't; when Emily had mentioned the idea, Jo had killed it on the spot.

'A complete waste of two weeks,' had been her comment.

'But Jo, it would be relaxing to get waited on hand and foot,' Emily had protested. They had been cooking dinner; Jo chopping tomatoes for a salad, Emily stirring a casserole with a wooden spoon.

'There's nothing to see in the Adirondacks; we've been there half-a-dozen times. We'd be bored out of our minds.'

Emily tasted the tip of the wooden spoon. 'I don't know,' she said musingly. 'I wouldn't mind resting for a couple of weeks.'

'Well, I'd go berserk,' Jo countered, emphasising her statement with an emphatic shake of her head. 'Now, the Rockies really appeal to me. Think of nights sleeping in mountain air and the sights from the mountain trails. I've heard it's fantastic!'

'But you know that I'm not crazy about . . .'

Jo hadn't even listened. 'Come on, Em, you know you'll love it.'

After Jo had gone on in the same forceful vein for some minutes, Emily had reluctantly agreed with her, but now Jo winced as she recalled the conversation. Had she really sounded so bossy and dictatorial? She wished she had listened more to Emily and had been more sensitive to her likes and dislikes. She was just so accustomed to getting her own way that she had simply ignored what Emily had said. Jo ran her hands through her tangled curls and vowed that the next time she'd do what Emily suggested. It would only be fair.

Jo was so immersed in her troubled thoughts that she failed to hear the sharp snap of a twig in the bushes that ringed the campfire or to see the tall figure that stopped just short of the clearing.

'A penny for your thoughts, New York,' a deep male voice said.

Startled, Jo's head flew up and she scrambled to her feet at the sight of a tall, lean figure in jeans, leaning nonchalantly against a tree. 'I ...' she stammered. 'Who? ... How did you know I came from New York?'

'We met today. Don't you remember?' The stranger stepped farther into the clearing and Jo suddenly recognised him.

Actually, they had met, or rather passed, each other twice earlier that afternoon. The first time had been in the doorway to the admissions office of the hospital. Jo had been too concerned with Emily to do much more than notice that the man who was so politely opening the door was extremely attractive. The next time had been in the hospital parking lot when she had turned her head to back her car out of its space and seen the stranger walking behind her. He had bowed slightly and tipped the edge of his broad-brimmed cowboy hat in a farewell gesture. He must have seen her licence plates then.

Now, she saw that her earlier assessment of him had been correct. The stranger was very good-looking in that rugged way of a man who has spent a great deal of time outdoors. He had thick blond hair that captured glints from the fire in its strands; grey eyes that were wide-set; a firm, straight nose; and a dark-gold moustache that lay above a well-formed mouth. There were lines around his eyes from squinting at the sun, and his skin had a bronzed sheen as if he rarely wore the white cowboy hat which was swinging from his fingers.

'Yes,' she said. 'I remember now.'

'Mind if I join you?'

Actually, Jo preferred her solitude. She wasn't

worried that he might be dangerous, but by nature she was wary of strangers. Still, she couldn't exactly say no, so she gave a slight shrug. 'If you want to.'

One blond eyebrow rose in a mocking arch. 'You're not too friendly, New York. This isn't Fifth Avenue, you know.'

'I don't live in Manhattan,' Jo retorted. 'I live in upstate New York.' It always annoyed her when strangers assumed that anyone from New York came from the City, as if it were the only part of the state that counted.

The eyebrow arched perceptibly higher. 'Pardon me.' And his eyes ran over Jo in a distinctly derisive way, encompassing the outline of her breasts through the thin windbreaker, the jeans that fitted snugly over her slim hips, the long length of her legs, and the squared toes of her boots.

Jo flushed, realising that she had sounded more impolite than she had intended. 'Be my guest.' She waved a hand at the fire and sat down again.

The stranger squatted down by the fire and the flames sent flickering lights across his face, playing across its hard planes and laying a sensuous shadow across his lower lip. Jo, fascinated in spite of herself, reluctantly looked away and back into the embers of the fire. Other women might easily fall for those good looks, but Jo didn't like to be part of a crowd.

'What are you doing so far from home?' he asked lazily, stretching his hands out to the fire.

'Vacationing. We thought we'd go to the Stampede and then on to Banff,' Jo replied.

'We . . .?'

'My sister was with me, but she broke her leg.' Jo turned to him. 'And you?'

'I'm from Calgary, but my nephew and I were camping here. He broke his arm, actually his elbow. It might require surgery.'

Jo couldn't remember seeing a boy with the stranger when she was at the hospital, but then she couldn't remember very much from that afternoon except Emily's pale face and pain-filled eyes. 'Poor kid,' she said sympathetically.

The stranger gave a grunt of agreement. 'Mind if I put another log on?' he asked, pointing to the fire.

'No.'

The stranger expertly rearranged the wood in the fire and placed another branch across the flames. 'Aren't you a little nervous, being up here by yourself?'

'Why should I be?' Jo gave him a narrowed glance through her dark eyelashes and prepared herself for the inevitable male chauvinistic remark about being a woman in an isolated spot, trying to do a man's job.

'This is grizzly bear country.'

It wasn't quite the remark, she had expected, but Jo still didn't like the stranger's intimation that she was ignorant of the dangers of camping in the Rockies. She knew that the wooded slopes of the mountains were the hunting ground for several dangerous species, 'Frankly,' she said sharply, 'I worry more about human predators than animal ones.'

To her surprise, the stranger threw her an appreciative glance. 'What do you do for a living, New York?'

'I'm a geologist,' Jo said, expecting to throw him off; geology was an unusual profession for a woman. 'I teach at a community college and do research.'

Again to her surprise, the stranger didn't look a bit startled. 'What type of geology?' he asked.

As Jo explained that her particular field of speciality was environmental geology, she found herself disconcerted by the stranger's apparently sincere interest. She had rarely met a man who could adjust to the fact that her fashion model looks hid an intelligent mind that operated quite successfully in a man's world. Men, she had discovered, preferred to think that nothing more existed behind a pretty woman's smile than fluffy thoughts and an occasional trivial opinion. '. . . and my last paper was on coal reclamation in Pennsylvania,' she concluded.

The stranger raised an eyebrow. 'Is that why you're camping here?'

Jo shrugged. 'A working holiday, I suppose. This area is a prime example of corporate pillage. Wyatt Mining is destroying the countryside, acres and acres of forest ruined by their policy of strip mining and careless dumping. The slag heaps near Crow's Nest Pass are an obscenity.' Her voice ended on a more vehement note than she had intended.

'You're going to write about them?' The stranger gave her a curious look.

'I'd like a chance to interview Conrad Wyatt,' she said grimly. 'I don't see how the man can be blind to what's happening, although he may be too old-fashioned or ignorant or uncaring to feel responsible. Big business has to clean up its act, and Wyatt Mining should be reclaiming the land it has already destroyed.'

'Very impassioned,' the stranger said dryly, staring into the fire.

Jo looked suspiciously at his enigmatic profile, wondering if he were the type of person who sided with business interests. 'I don't see anything wrong with being impassioned about something as important as saving our natural resources from a ruthless plunderer,' she retorted.

'Those are strong words to say about a man you don't know.'

'I don't have to *know* him,' Jo snapped back. 'I can see what he's doing.' Jo was reluctant to put her feelings into words; they were too strong, too emotional to be spoken before a stranger.

Jo had become a geologist for many reasons. She loved the outdoors; as a child she had always preferred the summers when she played outside all day and could spend the night in a tent in the back yard. As an adult she hated to be confined to rooms, houses and buildings, and even in the winter her bedroom window was left open so she could breathe the cold fresh air as she slept.

If the stranger had asked, Jo would have told him that something very elemental in her nature was bound up with land and trees and sky. Some people had obsessions with art or jewellery or food; Jo had an obsession with nature. She was, of course, sensible enough to realise that people needed houses and stores and cities, but she strongly objected to the way big business tended to tear apart a landscape without any concern for its integrity, for the animals that lived there or for the way the earth would heal. When she had driven by the Wyatt Mining coal fields and seen the holes that were dug out of the mountainside and heard the rumble of heavy trucks as they drove across dusty earth that had once been green and fertile, Jo had suffered from a familiar sense of outrage. She hadn't intended to work on her vacation, but neither could she turn her back on such blatant devastation.

She belonged to a small coterie of people from every professional field who were concerned with the environment. During the past few years, their main effort had been to change the law so that companies like Wyatt Mining could be held responsible for their actions. Their collected voice was small as yet, but Jo hoped that in time the pressure they imposed would have its effect. Still, it was an uphill battle, and as she stared into leaping flames of her campfire, Jo wondered with a sense of defeat whether the report she intended to write on the Canadian Rockies would have any impact at all.

The stranger seemed to think it prudent to change the subject. 'Look, there's a thunderstorm coming tonight, and I just thought you'd like to know that I'm camping just over the hill and . . .'

The implication that she couldn't cope on her own made Jo's hackles rise. 'I can manage,' she said.

'Well, just in case you spring a leak.'

'The tent is new, expensive and in perfect condition.'

The stranger ignored her. 'And feel in need of company.'

Jo lifted her chin defiantly. 'I didn't *ask* for help or company,' she retorted. 'In fact, I enjoy being by myself.'

The stranger turned from the fire to give Jo the full benefit of an appraising look from his hard grey eyes. 'Stubborn, aren't you? Have you ever been caught in a mountain storm?'

'It won't be the first time.' A suspicion entered Jo's head. 'I don't suppose it's a coincidence that, in all this territory,' and she waved her hand into the darkness towards the vast range of mountains, 'you and I managed to end up virtually on top of each other.'

The stranger gave her a mocking grin. 'A delightful position. Why don't we try it?'

Jo glared at him. Typical, she thought, that he would twist what she had said into a sexual connotation. '*Did* you follow me?' she asked him point-blank.

'If you promise not to shoot, I'll confess that I saw your car down by the gully. It struck me that you were alone and in a foreign country and could possibly use some help.'

'How kind of you,' Jo said scathingly. 'Unfortunately, I'm extremely capable of taking care of myself.'

'I noticed,' he drawled, slowly unwinding his long length from the ground and pulling himself to his full height.

Jo looked deliberately away from him and back to the fire. 'Goodbye,' she said in a curt voice.

'Sweet dreams, New York.'

The crackle of leaves told Jo that he had gone and she breathed a sigh of relief. Poking at the dying fire with a stick, she pondered his real reason for camping so near to her. She scoffed at the story he had told her which, she thought, had about as many holes in it as a piece of Swiss cheese. Why would a stranger care how she survived the night? It was more likely that he had another motive. A man with his looks would be accustomed to female conquests, and Jo strongly suspected that a cosy one-night stand in his tent had been at the back of his mind.

In that case, he had the wrong woman. Jo yawned and stood up, stretching her arms over her head. She wasn't insensitive to the spark of sexuality that had sprung up between them, but she was quite capable of dousing it. She'd learned, by a hard lesson, that reaching out for that spark, yielding to it, could burn her, and the experience had been far too painful to forget. Let the stranger look elsewhere for a joyride, she thought grimly and with great satisfaction. He wasn't going to find it with her.

Jo banked the coals in the fire in preparation for the morning's meal and began to gather up all the items left in the campsite. Only a few things could be left to the mercy of the weather, and Jo preferred to keep her possessions in the tent with her where they would stay high and dry. She could hear a rumbling sound in the sky, far away but distinct enough to hint at the coming storm. The stranger's forecast seemed to have been accurate.

Once inside the small tent, she pulled the outside flap down and zipped up the canvas door. She felt fairly secure with a trench dug around the circumference of the tent, the ground sheet below her, and the canvas taut and waterproof over her head. The tent was, as she had told the stranger, a new one, bought especially for this trip. It was a pup tent designed for two, not large enough to stand up in, but very lightweight and easy to pack. Although it hadn't proved itself in the rain yet, Jo was confident in its protection. The salesman who sold it to them had insisted that it was top of the line, a statement reinforced by its high price.

She slipped out of her jeans and sweater, but kept on her blouse. Her sleeping bag was so warm and snug that she needed only the lightest covering when she slept. She climbed into it, rolled up a towel to be her pillow and then blew out the kerosene lamp she had brought in. The flashlight was in the sleeping bag with her in case of an emergency.

With the light doused, the inside of the tent was

completely black, and now that Jo could no longer see, the sounds outside the tent became even more noticeable. The wind roared in the trees and she could hear branches striking one another and leaves being blown against the tent. The coming storm would have upset Emily but it didn't frighten Jo. Although she knew there was no danger, she liked the sensation of living on the edge of disaster, of having only the thin membrane of the tent between her and the wind and rain. There was a feeling akin to triumph in being warm and cosy in the tent while the storm raged futilely outside.

The blackness, the sound of the wind and Jo's exhaustion from the events of the day combined to close her eyes almost immediately, and she fell into a deep sleep with dreams too fragmentary to remember. Outside the tent, heavy clouds, generating electrical currents of enormous voltage, formed in the sky. The winds grew wilder and soon heavy drops of rain began to strike the trees, the ground and the canvas over Jo's head. Lightning slashed the sky and thunder rolled across the horizon shaking the earth, but still Jo slept, her eyes shut tight as if enormous weights pressed them down.

A small hole at the top of the tent that had opened earlier when Jo had unwittingly packed a corner seam tight against the pointed edge of a tent nail, widened under pressure from the driving rain. Water began to fall through the hole and form a spreading pool on the tent's floor, slowly but surely soaking everything in its path.

In her sleep Jo struggled to stay warm and tried to wriggle deeper and deeper into her sleeping bag, but her restlessness finally woke her. To her horror, she found that the bottom of her sleeping bag was wet, her feet and legs were freezing cold and the floor of the tent was covered by a film of water. The beam of her flashlight revealed the extent of the disaster, and she sat up with a groan of dismay. Her sleeping bag was uninhabitable;

the jeans and sweater that she had left on the floor of the tent were soaked; and worst of all, her matches lay directly in the trail of the water.

Jo had a reputation for having a level head. The panicky feeling that had first come over her slowly dissipated as she fought to be practical, logical, and pragmatic. She weighed her choices carefully. Staying in the tent meant risking a case of pneumonia since all of her warm clothing was useless. Jo cursed her earlier efficiency; without Emily to help carry the camping gear, she had cut back on all her personal belongings. All that remained in her waterproof backpack was a pair of shorts and a change of socks. Hiking back to the car meant a three mile walk in the dark and pouring rain with only a poncho to protect her. With great reluctance, Jo faced the hard facts. Her only salvation was the stranger. She shone the flashlight on her watch and found that it was two o'clock in the morning. She wondered how he was sleeping in the middle of the storm. Probably like a baby in a warm, dry tent.

Jo could have cried with frustration. The very last place on earth that she wanted to be was in the stranger's tent. The thought of the smug expression on his face when he saw her arrive, wet and bedraggled, made her grind her teeth together. And how big a tent did he have? If it was the size of hers, then it would be a very cosy arrangement. Too cosy. Then it occurred to her that they would have to share a sleeping bag. That, Jo decided emphatically, was the clincher. She'd rather brave the dark, the rain and the three mile hike.

With the thin beam of her flashlight, Jo located her backpack and pulled on her shorts and poncho. The socks were warm and dry as were her waterproof boots. When she was finally dressed, she unzipped the canvas door and pulled aside the flap. Rain, cold and piercing, struck her full in the face and she pulled back quickly, letting the flap fall into place again. It was far worse outside than she had anticipated.

Jo shivered, feeling the cold sink into her bones. The

low height of the tent forced her into a kneeling position, and her bare knees were submerged in water. She was quickly beginning to feel sorry for herself. The hike to the car was out of the question, staying in the tent was impossible and the only alternative was the stranger. She was, she saw unhappily, going to have to swallow her pride and beg for his help.

Jo slowly crawled out of the tent into a sea of mud and began to walk, her heart in her throat, her flashlight throwing a thin beam on to the ground. It was black and cold. Overhead, the tangled branches of the pines whipped and groaned in the wind, and some needles, freed by a sudden gust, flew into Jo's face, making her flinch. Her boots sank in an inch every time she took a step and the hood of her poncho kept blowing off her head. By the time she finally reached the stranger's tent after a twisted trek through the trees, she had lost her last shred of dignity. She couldn't wait to get inside and see the face of another human being, be it friendly or hostile, smug or welcoming.

'Hello!' she yelled, crouching down before the flap of his tent. It wasn't much bigger than hers, but that didn't matter any more. At least it was dry. She could hear the zipper being pulled down, and then the flap was pulled aside. A flashlight beamed into her face and Jo blinked.

'A social call?' asked the deep voice in an exaggerated drawl.

'Will you please let me in?' she pleaded. 'It's wet out here.'

The flap was held open and Jo quickly crawled into the tent, sighing with relief when her bare legs encountered the dry floor. She carefully stripped off her dripping wet poncho and pushed it into a corner. She was just unlacing her boots when the stranger lit a match to the kerosene lamp, illuminating the entire tent with a yellow glow. Jo glanced at him and then quickly looked away. He had slept, it seemed, almost nude except for a pair of dark briefs. The flickering light of the lamp was reflected in the bronzed skin of his shoulders and glinted off the golden hairs on his chest and muscular legs. His silvery blond hair, dishevelled by sleep, tumbled about his forehead.

He was lying on top of his sleeping bag, propped up on one elbow. 'A plumbing problem in your new tent?'

Jo ate humble pie. 'It's leaking.'

'You do look damp.' He mockingly eyed the wet tendrils of Jo's hair and the drops of water dripping off her legs.

Jo fought with a shoelace. 'It's unbelievable out there. Who would ever think it could rain so hard?'

The stranger at least had the grace to refrain from the obvious comment that he had told her so. 'You'd better get dry,' he said, noting the way she was shivering in her thin cotton blouse and skimpy shorts. He reached for a towel, the muscles moving powerfully under his sleek skin, and threw it at her. 'You'll catch pneumonia if you don't.'

Jo began to rub her hair, thankful that the towel obscured his view of her face. She was feeling embarrassed and humiliated when she compared the nasty way she had refused his offer of help and his present generosity. She wouldn't blame him if he wanted to rub her nose in her own imcompetence. Jo began to formulate the most sincere apology she could think of for her bad manners the evening before, when she happened to glance up and catch the stranger's expression as he watched her dry her hair.

There were euphemisms for looks like that, but Jo preferred to be frank with herself. Desire glinted in the grey eyes shaded by thick golden lashes; lust gave a sensuous curve to his lips. Jo had a sudden image how she looked to him, sitting cross-legged, her arms raised to her head, the cotton blouse sticking damply to her unconfined breasts. The half-formulated apology vanished from her mind. She now remembered his reasons for wanting to be so helpful, and bells of caution rang in her head.

'Do you have an extra blanket?' she asked.

His smile was sardonic. 'Never pack one.'

He obviously knew what Jo had in mind and found it highly amusing. She rubbed her hair furiously. 'Could I borrow your pants and a sweater?'

'The sleeping bag is made of down,' he countered smoothly. 'You'll suffocate in heavy clothes.'

Jo looked at him through the tangle of her black curls. 'I prefer to sleep on the ground,' she said coldly.

'You'll be miserable trying to sleep that way,' he said lazily.

'It's better than . . .' Jo bit her tongue.

'Better than joining me in the sleeping bag?' he supplied for her. 'And lying on a comfortable air mattress?'

'I'd prefer . . .' she repeated.

The stranger shifted impatiently. 'Look, if it's any comfort to you, the only thing I'm concerned with is a good night's sleep. The tent's too small for one of us to be uncomfortable without the other being aware of it, and the only way you're going to be able to sleep is on the air mattress with me.'

Jo knew he was right, but the idea of sharing the same sleeping bag with that distracting masculine body was terrifying. 'If you don't mind . . .'

Stone grey eyes drilled right through her. 'I do mind; I'd like to get some sleep. And if it's your virtue that's worrying you, frankly, an unwilling seduction isn't at the top of my priority list at the moment.'

Jo threw him a look from her amber eyes that would have put a lesser man six foot under.

The stranger slid into his sleeping bag and reached for the kerosene lamp. 'It's now or never,' he said firmly.

Jo made the distasteful decision instantaneously. Wordlessly, she climbed in after him, as he blew the kerosene light out, plunging the tent into darkness. Outside the storm continued unabated, the wind whistling around the corners of the tent, rain beating against the canvas.

'Cosy, isn't it?' the deep masculine voice said softly in her ear.

It was Joe's thought precisely. In order to fit into the sleeping bag, the two of them were curled together, her back to his front, like a pair of nesting spoons. They touched at several intimate points; her lower back curved against his flat stomach, her bare calf grazed his knee, the heel of one foot rested against his ankle. He gave off a warmth that banished the chill of the previous hour and Jo had the urge to snuggle closer. Fighting it, she tried to wiggle away.

'Uncomfortable?' His mocking tone indicated that he guessed her inhibitions.

Jo cleared her throat. 'Just trying to find the right position.'

'There is only one position for two people in a sleeping bag. Here, I'll show you.'

One muscular arm curled around her waist, pulling her closer to him, so that their bodies formed two interlocking S shapes. Tired from her loss of sleep and the last hour's struggle, Jo yielded to his strength, allowing her body to curve against his and, despite herself, enjoying the protection of his hard muscles. How Emily would laugh, Jo thought drowsily, if she could see her sister sleeping in the arms of a man that she barely knew and didn't like. As Jo slipped into an exhausted sleep, her last thought was even more depressing. She didn't, she realised, even know his name.

CHAPTER TWO

Jo awoke to the cry of a raucous crow swooping down from the sky and sleepily opened her eyes. The storm of the night before had dissipated, and the leaves of trees overhead were making dappled shadows on the tent's canvas roof. She closed her eyes again and listened drowsily to the sounds of the forest; the chatter of squirrels and the rustle of a breeze in low-lying branches. She yawned, stretching as she did, her arms high above her head, her back arched into a lithe curve. She always enjoyed waking up in the morning when she was camping. There was that invigorating sense of being outdoors, the cleansing feel of the cool mountain air, the . . .

Clock! Jo's eyes flew open at a sound that bore no resemblance to anything in nature. The clicking noise came again, this time more loudly, and sounding very much like a spoon or utensil moving against the side of a metal pot. She turned over and found herself staring, bird's eye level, at a neatly folded pile of unfamiliar clothes; a checked shirt, blue jeans with a black leather belt and a set of men's briefs.

Memories of the night before came flooding back in excruciating and thorough detail. She had fallen asleep in the stranger's arms, and she distinctly remembered the sensation of his hand spread across the curve of her hips and their bare legs touching right down to their toes. Jo sat up hurriedly and looked around the tent. It was empty, as was the place in the sleeping bag beside her, and she flushed to think that she'd been sleeping so heavily that she hadn't even roused when the stranger had got up that morning. How had she looked to him? she wondered, with her black hair tangled around her head, her face unguarded and vulnerable, and then squirmed with embarrassment at the thought of those grey eyes watching her as she slept. She hastily climbed out of the sleeping bag, straightening her clothes as she did so and pulling her fingers through her hair in a futile effort to make herself presentable.

The stranger's back was to her when she unzipped the tent and looked out of its front flap. He was kneeling before a campfire that crackled with fresh wood, the occasional spark shooting high in the air, and he wore only brief white shorts and no shirt, the long line of his brown muscles gleaming in the early morning sun, its rays picking up gold in the thick strands of his hair. He pulled a pot of coffee off the grate that he had placed on two rocks over the fire, and the appetising aroma of fresh-perked coffee filled the air, making Jo's hungry stomach rumble in protest.

'Sleep well, New York?'

Jo stepped completely outside the tent. 'Like a log,' she said.

He smiled lazily. 'You didn't even wake up when I crawled over you.'

Jo tried to ignore the rush of blood to her cheeks. She didn't like being reminded that she had spent the night in his arms. 'You don't have to feed me breakfast,' she protested as he poured the coffee into two waiting mugs. 'I'll just go back to my campsite and . . .'

'What's your hurry?' The smoky grey eyes appraised her, from the halo of dark hair, over her tumbled shirt and down to the long, shapely length of her bare legs.

'I . . .'

'Correct me if I'm wrong, New York, but it seems to me that people from your part of the world can't ever relax. You're jumpier than a cat on a hot tin roof.'

'I told you,' Jo said, her eyebrows drawing together in a frown, 'I'm not from Manhattan.'

The stranger stood up and handed her the steaming mug. 'You're an Easterner,' he said. 'It's the same breed.'

Jo glanced up at him, noticed that even at this hour

he was devastatingly handsome despite the blond stubble that lined his lean cheeks and looked away, sipping at her coffee. 'You sound prejudiced.'

A muscle leaped in his jaw, but he answered nonchalantly. 'Just an observation on the species.'

'We're not any different than you are,' she said.

'No?' He glanced at her and then, taking a frying pan out of a pack, placed it over the fire. 'In my experience, people from your part of the world don't know how to slow down and savour life.'

His generalisations were rousing Jo's ire. 'Perhaps we get more accomplished that way,' she said sarcastically.

'You're a prime example,' he said, ignoring her mockery. 'You're here on a holiday but you still want to work.'

'I told you—it's a working holiday.'

He shrugged his broad, tanned shoulders. 'The point of a vacation is to get away from a job and responsibilities. Give your mind a rest.'

Jo glanced curiously at his chiselled profile. 'Is that what you're doing?' she asked.

'I was taking a few days away from work,' he acknowledged.

'And what do you do?'

'Manage a company.'

'Which one?' she persisted.

He gave her a knowing grin. 'I'm on holiday,' he said, 'and I don't mix business with pleasure. Scrambled eggs okay with you?'

'I really don't think . . .'

'Do you have to catch a train?' he asked sarcastically.

'I'm not hungry,' she lied.

He cocked a dark gold eyebrow as her stomach gave a particularly loud rumble. 'Sounds like starvation to me,' he said.

Jo put her cup down on a rock beside the fire. 'It can wait,' she replied haughtily.

'You're as tough as nails, New York, aren't you?'

Later, as she pulled open the glass doors of the Pincher Creek hospital and entered its white tiled lobby, Jo shrugged off the stranger's words as inconsequential. She'd left him right after that, pulling on her socks and hiking boots, saying a brief farewell and heading back to her wet campsite, all the while ignoring a sardonic gaze that implied she was cutting off her nose to spite her face. Jo still didn't know his name, but she didn't much care. What was one blond stranger in the course of her life? She'd met many handsome men, all of whom had been intimidated by her poise and professional competence. She was used to being called tough by men that she worked with or competed against. They thought it was an insult, but Jo had always found it a compliment. Being tough was one of her best characteristics; it had gotten her through some very hard times.

Take this morning, for instance. If she'd been some weepy female who cracked at the least sign of strain, she would never have survived. She'd returned to her tent to discover a small pool on the floor of her tent, some very damp clothes and sopping wet sleeping bag. She's strung up a line to hang up the sleeping bag and wrung out her clothes, laying them on some stones to dry. Breakfast was plain bread and a can of cold beans, not the most appetising meal, but by the time Jo sat down to eat it, she was beyond caring that it was anything but sustenance.

Two hours later she had hiked back to the car with her damp bedroll and backpack and then driven to town where she found a shoemaker who agreed to stitch up her tent and was kind enough, when he saw her plight, to allow her to hang her damp things over the fence that enclosed the back of his shop. Fortunately, there was no sign of another storm. The Alberta sky was a clear blue without even the smallest cloud, and the sun shone down unhindered over the buildings of Pincher Creek and the surrounding low hills which were covered by long, brown prairie grasses. In the distance,

Jo could see the Rockies, their peaks jutting into the sky; massive, grey and monolithic.

Her back and arms ached by the time she reached the hospital, but Jo ignored the pain as she stepped off the elevator on to the floor that housed her sister's room. She felt apprehensive and jittery, wondering if she'd find Emily in the condition that she'd left her, her small face almost as white as the sheets she was lying on and her mouth pinched with pain. She had felt so helpless after the accident, sitting uselessly in the waiting room while the nurses and doctors had come and gone, their faces impersonal, their kind smiles merely polite. She was accustomed to taking charge, to solving problems and to being in control. It had hurt to sit on a hard chair, surrounded by old, torn magazines, and feel Emily's distress as her own.

So afraid was she that Emily would be lying in bed, doped with sedatives and still racked with pain, that Jo was gritting her teeth as she turned into the door of the hospital room. To her utter shock, she found her sister sitting up against a bank of pillows, her cheeks flushed pink and her mouth curved into a smile. Emily's soft blonde hair had been brushed until it gleamed and fell to her shoulders in a shining curtain. She was wearing a royal blue robe that matched the colour of her eyes, and she didn't look anything like a hospital patient or the girl who had cracked her ankle in three places the day before. If it weren't for the hospital bed with its metal sides, the indentification bracelet on her wrist and the bulky cast on her ankle, Jo would have thought that Emily was merely entertaining a guest in the privacy of her home.

A dark haired young man lounged at the foot of her bed. He was dressed in a pair of pyjamas, a dark red bathrobe and a pair of leather slippers, one arm making rapid motions in the air as he mimicked a conversation. '. . . "and here's the bedpan," the nurse said. You know which one she is, the one with a face like a gorgon. But I can walk, I protested, but to no avail. "Young man," she said pompously, "it's against hospital rules for a new patient to be ambulatory." ' He dragged out the word, am-bu-la-tor-y, and Emily laughed with delight.

Jo cleared her throat and their heads turned.

'Jo!' Emily exclaimed.

Jo walked in, ignored the young man who was eying her with lively curiosity and, giving Emily a hug, sat down in the chair by her bed. 'I'm sorry,' she said, 'I had to get the tent repaired and couldn't get here any earlier this morning.'

Emily had no interest in their tent. 'Paul, this is my sister, Jo,' she said enthusiastically. 'Jo, this is Paul Wyatt. He's here because he broke his elbow and had to have a pin put in.'

The young man gave her a welcoming grin and pointed to the sling that held his right arm close to his chest. 'Fell down the side of a mountain while my uncle and I were camping,' he said cheerfully.

Jo stared at the young man and saw something in his face that made a sinking feeling develop in the pit of her stomach. He was dark, but he had a line of jaw and incisive curve to his mouth that she had seen elsewhere. She rapidly ran through an assorted number of disturbing facts; there was the resemblance, the stranger's mention of a nephew with a broken elbow, his admission that he ran a company, the way he had changed the subject when she talked about mining. She hoped against hope that the emerging pattern could be proven wrong, but finally arrived at the only possible conclusion.

'Did you say ... Wyatt?' she asked faintly.

Paul gave her a snappy, military salute with his left hand. 'That's me.'

'And ... you have an uncle?'

'Last time I looked,' he agreed cheerfully. 'Conrad; blond, tall and adorned with a dashing moustache.'

The sinking feeling in Jo's stomach resolved itself into a definite hollow as she desperately tried to recall all the things she had said to the stranger the night

before when she hadn't been aware that he was Conrad
Wyatt. She had been pompous and argumentative.
She'd been nasty and insulting. She remembered, with
agonising clarity, calling him a ruthless plunderer. Jo
flushed as she realised how he must have been laughing
at her and groaned inwardly when she contemplated the
ruin of her plans.

She'd had such a clever strategy; at least that's how
she saw it. After seeing the Wyatt mine operations, she
had devised a plan for interviewing Conrad without
letting him know her intentions or her identity. If he
was like most mining executives, he wouldn't meet with
an environmental specialist if he could help it. Jo's
scheme had included passing herself off as a visiting
geologist with an interest in mines, rather than a
crusader who planned to publish an article about the
way Wyatt Mining was tearing up the mountains with
no thought of reclamation.

Some of her dismay must have shown in her face
because Emily was staring at her in astonishment and
Paul asked, 'Have you met him?'

Jo hurriedly shook her head in negation and, forcing
her mind off the subject of Conrad Wyatt, turned to
Emily. 'How's your ankle?' she asked.

Paul deserved high marks for sensitivity. Realising
that Jo wanted to be alone with her sister, he stood up
and gave them a sweeping bow. 'Until we meet again,
Emily of the broken leg.'

Emily gave him an enchanted smile. 'See you later,
Paul,' and then when he had gone, she turned to Jo and
sighed. 'Isn't he nice? He came in this morning after his
X-rays and said he was looking for a comrade in plaster.
We started talking; he lives in Calgary and . . .'

Jo ignored her sister's rush of words. 'Did the doctor
come by this morning?' she asked. 'Did he say anything
about when you'll be able to leave?'

Emily's face clouded, and Jo learned the disheartening
facts. The ankle still throbbed with pain and, although
the doctor was of the opinion that the discomfort would

disappear in a few days, he was adamant that Emily stay in the hospital to the end of the week and then remain in bed for several more weeks. Crutches would be the next step and, when the full-leg cast was taken off and a smaller one put on, Emily would be able to get around with a cane. Full recovery, he had estimated, would take about six weeks to two months.

'Two months!' Jo said in dismay.

Emily's mouth twisted and Jo could see that the bubbly exterior she had shown to Paul masked a considerable amount of apprehension. 'I know,' she said glumly, staring down at her hands and twisting a sheet in her slender fingers. 'I've ruined our holiday.'

Jo was quick to reassure her. 'I don't mind that, Em. It's just that I hate to see you immobilised for such a long period of time. But don't worry about it, we'll manage.'

Emily looked up unhappily. 'You mean, you'll have to manage. It seems like you're always looking after me.'

'I don't mind. Really.' Jo gave her an encouraging smile.

Emily stretched uncomfortably. 'I feel like such a burden.'

'Don't be silly!' Jo protested in a shocked voice. 'You could never be a burden.'

Emily gave a helpless shrug and looked away from Jo towards the window that looked towards the prairie, the land stretching like a golden blanket towards the horizon where it met the vast curve of blue sky. 'I didn't sleep well last night,' she said. 'I thought a lot about you and me and the kind of life we have together.'

There was something in Emily's voice that made Jo suddenly tense.

'And I came to the conclusion,' Emily went on, 'that it isn't right for you to be supporting me and taking care of me as if I were still a child. I have to grow up sometime.'

'We're sisters; we belong together,' Jo objected. 'I

don't mind helping out with the expenses. I earn more than you do.'

Emily turned back and gave Jo a beseeching look. 'It isn't normal,' she said. 'Don't you see that? We're both adults and should be living separate lives. You should be married, Jo. I've often thought that I was one of the reasons why you and Douglas broke up. He probably saw more of me than he wanted to and . . .'

Jo had stiffened at the mention of Douglas' name. 'You weren't a part of it,' she said.

'But, Jo, I was always with you and . . .'

Jo cut her off. 'There were other reasons.'

Emily knew better than to pursue a topic that her sister so obviously found abhorrent. 'Still,' she said. 'You haven't gone out with anyone since and it's been almost three years.'

'I'm not interested in men.'

'You shouldn't condemn the whole species because of Douglas,' Emily insisted.

Both sisters looked at one another in mute remembrance of Jo's unhappiness, and then Jo shrugged her shoulders lightly as if none of it mattered. 'I don't,' she said. 'There are lots of other fish in the sea. I just haven't met anyone interesting in a long time.'

Emily shook her head in disbelief. 'I know you're lonely,' she said gently, 'and living with me isn't the right answer.'

Jo drove away from the hospital later, disturbed and upset by Emily's words. She had never imagined that her sister was uncomfortable with their living arrangements; she'd always thought it suited them to a T, and she didn't at all mind contributing extra to their fund of housekeeping money. She was older and far more established in her career than Emily. It was only logical that she earned more and should pay a heftier share of the rent, and she didn't think their living together was unnatural at all. Lots of people shared apartments with friends, sometimes even strangers. Jo much preferred being with her sister.

And Emily's suggestion that she was lonely was pure nonsense, of course. She wasn't lonely; in fact, far from it. Her life was full, right up to the hilt with work and Emily. Even Prudence, who had gotten a job but never remarried, looked to Jo for advice and reassurance. How could Emily say that she was lonely? Loneliness was a state of mind that Jo associated with old people, widows and divorcees like her mother, who had spent months after their father had left weeping about how alone she was.

Jo had often thought that being single was not necessarily synonymous with being lonely. It merely depended on how it was handled. Some women sought out male companionship because they were afraid to be alone; others, like Jo, had realised that being single meant being independent, and her freedom was something she prized very highly. Her affair with Douglas had taught Jo in no uncertain terms that she didn't want to be the possession of some man.

In a perverse sort of way, she had come to value the heartbreak Douglas had caused her. It had been a trial by fire and she'd come through unscathed and able to hold her head up high, having learned the hard way that love is an overrated commodity that causes nothing but a despicable weakness in the afflicted sufferer. She knew how it felt, first-hand, to be hurt by a man and had vowed to herself never to let it happen again. Forewarned is forearmed; and Jo had been wary of other men ever since, having built a wall around her heart that was impregnable. She felt safer that way; there would be no more pain, no more tears, no more self-recriminations. Jo considered herself healed, although she knew that the scars remained, sensitive to the slightest pressure.

For the next few days, Jo continued a daily routine of camping and visiting Emily. The tent had been easily repaired and her equipment finally dried. She picked a campsite in the lower part of the mountains, an area that wasn't attractive enough to entice other solitary campers. She never saw Conrad Wyatt again although she always had an uneasy feeling that he'd pop up at the most unlikely time and place. But when he hadn't appeared by the third day, Jo breathed a sigh of relief, glad that she wouldn't have to confront him and apologise for her unrestrained words.

Still, meeting him had a strange impact on her imagination. Jo found that she no longer dropped off to sleep at night with the ease of someone who has spent the day outdoors. She tossed and turned in her sleeping bag, stared up at the dark peak of her tent and listened for hours to the mountain wind blow around its corners. She had quite forgotten the pleasure of sleeping next to a male body and the comfort of being held in someone's arms. The sensations had awoken a whole set of longings and desires that Jo hadn't felt for years. She'd stifled the sensual part of her nature long ago, knowing how reckless it had made her, and she didn't welcome its return. She much preferred the cool rational use of her mind to the blind impulse of her emotions.

With a fierce determination, Jo tried to put Conrad Wyatt out of her mind. It was unfortunate that they'd met and she'd been so indiscreet, but the experience was over and done with. What she had to do was concentrate on the predicament that Emily had placed them in. There were the physical difficulties of moving Emily from Alberta to New York and the financial problem of finding enough cash for her plane ride back, not to mention the medical bills, the car insurance that would be due in September and their need for a new couch. The old one was falling apart, its springs breaking through the upholstery. Jo struggled and wrestled with the dilemma, tossing one plan out after another. She hated to borrow money from Prudence; her mother didn't have much anyway and Jo knew that a loan would have emotional strings attached. With growing dismay, Jo came to the conclusion that her only hope was to attempt, long-distance, an expensive and possibly ruinous loan from their bank.

Although her worries beset her, Jo didn't reveal any of them to Emily whose recovery was as slow as predicted. Since the swelling had gone down inside the cast, she was no longer suffering from pain, but she was still unable to put her weight on her foot and required the assistance of two people to manage the brief walk to the bathroom and back. Nevertheless her spirits were high and she often greeted Jo with a happy smile. As the week wore on, Jo came slowly to the realisation that nothing was curing Emily faster than the presence of a young, attractive male who was more than willing to keep her occupied.

Jo often found her with Paul. He was charming, fun and seemingly had an inexhaustible supply of banter and camaraderie. He and Emily had an ongoing rummy game which they alternated with an ongoing checkers match, all the while cracking jokes about the nurses, the doctors and the lousy meals and service. While Jo conceded that hospital life was boring, she was alarmed at the speed with which Emily had become attached to Paul. Although her sister had always made male friends easily, she had never been serious about any particular man. Paul seemed to affect her differently, and Jo sensed that Emily's feelings towards him were daily growing deeper.

As she watched the pair of them laughing and joking and noticed the way Emily's blue eyes softened when Paul was nearby, Jo worried about the future. The pain and weakness of Emily's injury had made her vulnerable to Paul's kindness, and Jo could see that her sister thought his attention went beyond mere friendship. She herself couldn't help being more objective; she saw Paul as being light-hearted and flirtatious, whiling away tedious hours with a pretty girl as a distraction. She was afraid that Emily was going to get hurt when her hospital stay was over and Paul bid her a very final farewell, but Jo found herself unable to issue any advice or warning. She simply didn't have the heart to dampen the happiness that made Emily's eyes shine or her smile come so readily.

Her distrust of Paul increased dramatically when she arrived one afternoon to find Emily barely able to greet her before bursting out with a half-cocked idea that she insisted would solve all their problems. Jo sat in disbelief as Emily, excited and flushed, outlined a scheme that could only have been dreamed up by Paul.

'Wait a minute,' Jo protested, stopping Emily's flow of words. 'Do you mean that Paul is inviting both of us to spend the next month in Calgary?'

Emily nodded, her blue eyes bright. 'He and his uncle live in a ranch twenty miles west of Calgary. He says that there's plenty of room in the house to accommodate us, and we won't have to worry about getting me back to New York until I can walk with a cane.'

Jo took a deep breath, sat back in the chair she'd placed beside Emily's bed and tried to dissuade her sister. She knew that she couldn't accept Paul's offer of hospitality. She never wanted to see Conrad again; one embarrassing encounter was enough.

'We can't do that,' she said, shaking her head.

'Why not?'

'We can't stay with people we don't know,' she protested.

'But we know Paul,' Emily pointed out.

Jo didn't bother to point out that *she* hardly knew Paul at all. 'I don't think a five day acquaintance means that you know someone, Em.'

Emily's mouth developed a stubborn line that Jo had never seen before. 'Paul has been wonderful to me. He's kind and generous and decent. Just because I haven't known him for my whole life doesn't mean that he's automatically a suspicious character.'

Jo tried a different tack. 'But we don't know his uncle, and besides, he may not want us.'

'Paul says that he told his uncle all about us and, in fact, it was *his* idea that we stay.'

Jo had a distasteful conviction that Conrad Wyatt had made just such an offer for the express purpose of rubbing her nose in her past humiliation. 'I think we'd be imposing,' she said. 'You're going to require special care and . . .'

Emily interrupted her. 'What were you planning, Jo? How were you going to get me back home?'

'I . . .' Jo stuttered slightly. 'I thought that you'd fly home and stay with Prudence.'

Emily looked at Jo as if she were crazy. 'She couldn't handle it.'

'Just because her apartment is tiny and she works all day doesn't mean . . .'

'I absolutely refuse,' Emily said, her small jaw clenched with determination. 'Prudence would drive me around the bend in two days.'

Unfortunately, Jo knew just what Emily was talking about. Prudence was easily flustered and lacked any commonsense. She also talked incessantly, her high voice in a constant, breathless monotone. Neither Jo nor Emily could stand their mother's conversation for any length of time. They loved her; they helped her when she had problems; but they tried to spend as little time as possible with her. They had, long ago, reluctantly agreed that their father was not necessarily the only guilty party in the break-up of their parents' marriage. He had lived with Prudence for ten years, which was nine years and three hundred and sixty-four days more than either Jo or Emily thought they could have survived.

'I know it's not the perfect solution,' Jo conceded reluctantly.

'I won't go.' Emily's voice was flat and unyielding.

Jo stared at her sister as if she was a stranger. She had never seen Emily so adamant before. She was usually easy-going and amenable to suggestion, willing to go along with Jo's wishes and desires. But now there was an unfamiliar fire in her wide blue eyes and an inflexible set to her mouth that made Jo hesitate.

'I don't think we have any other choice,' she finally said.

'We can go to the Wyatt's ranch,' Emily insisted. 'That's a perfectly good answer to our problems.'

Jo decided to stop beating around the bush and attack the real issue at hand. 'Just because Paul is paying attention to you now,' she said softly, 'doesn't mean that he'll be interested in you later.'

Emily had her own weapon. 'Paul is not Douglas.'

'Oh, Em . . .'

Her sister was immediately contrite. 'Jo, I'm sorry, but he isn't and you can't judge every man by your experience with one. I know that Paul might just be amusing himself while he's stuck in the hospital. But you know something?' She gave Jo a defiant glance. 'I'm willing to take the risk.'

Jo stared at Emily and felt as if she was gazing at a stranger. They had been so close in the past, agreeing on almost every issue and course of action. In the past Emily had concurred with Jo's belief that independence of body and spirit were essential for a woman's well-being, yet now she was prepared to throw herself on to the mercy of a man. It was obvious that her infatuation with Conrad's nephew was far deeper than Jo had suspected, and she had a strong desire to find Paul and wring his charming neck. He was, so obviously, leading Emily down a rosy path to emotional disaster.

'Em,' she said in a pleading voice, 'it would be crazy to . . .'

'If you don't want to go with me, Jo, then you can go back to New York on your own.'

Emily spoke in a low tone, but she faced Jo with the fire of determination blazing in her eyes. For the first time, Jo faced the uncomfortable truth that she'd lost influence over her sister, and she searched desperately for some argument that would convince Emily that she was mistaken.

'You'd stay all by yourself with strangers?' she asked incredulously.

Emily nodded emphatically, her soft blonde hair bouncing on the shoulders of her nightgown. 'Yes.'

Suddenly Jo had a flashback to the night before when she had sat in front of the campfire and felt guilty for all the tmes she had browbeaten Emily into doing what she had wanted to do. Jo had realised that she had gotten into the habit of trying to control Emily as if she were still a small child, and had vowed never to ride roughshod over Emily's wishes again. Yet, here she was, acting like some petty tyrant while her sister was rebelling, fighting for the freedom to make her own choices. Jo wished fervently that she could protect Emily from the sort of unhappiness she had suffered, but she unwillingly recognised the validity of an old truth: no one learns from another's experiences.

'Okay, Em,' she sighed. 'You win.'

Emily's face lit up. 'You don't mind?'

Jo shook her head wearily. She hadn't wanted to admit it to Emily, but Paul's suggestion was a godsend financially. By the time August was over, Emily would be out of a full-leg cast and able to withstand the long drive back to New York. That eliminated the cost of plane fare and the problem of her living alone while Jo drove the car home. There were still a host of other worries, but their solution could be put off for the month's hiatus.

She would just have to grit her teeth and bear her fears for Emily's emotional state in silence. She was older, wiser and more experienced but she couldn't help her sister. Perhaps, Emily had been right when she'd talked about growing up. Her sister had been singularly unmarked and unscathed in her encounters with men. She had never felt strongly about anyone and, consequently, she had a naïve vision of how the world worked. She expected that everyone would be kind, that the future was balmy and that she was invulnerable to hurt. Emily might have said that she was willing to risk

Paul's indifference, but Jo knew what lay under her words. Hope springs eternal, and the hope that her sister was nurturing was no exception. In her heart, Emily firmly believed that Paul reciprocated her feelings.

Emily leaned forward and touched her on the shoulder. 'Will you come with me, Jo? Please?'

Jo gave her sister a small smile. She may have agreed to let Emily enter into the lion's den, but she wasn't about to leave her there unaided. She didn't have to be back in New York until September either, and if Paul was the type to entertain ideas about seducing an innocent like her sister, he'd have to tangle with Jo first. She would do her best to protect Emily, even if it only meant running interference on Paul's designs and providing her sister with some reason and judgment if the relationship became too difficult for her to handle.

She had her suspicions about Conrad Wyatt's generous hospitality, but she would also have to keep them to herself. Jo had seen the look of lust in his eyes that night in the tent and was well aware that a spark of sensuality had been struck between them. If his invitation had been issued with the base motive of getting her into his house and then into his bed, then Jo determined that Conrad had a few surprises coming. She had supreme confidence in her ability to protect herself from the unwanted advances of men. They were an occupational hazard for a female geologist who looked as if she should be adorning the pages of a fashion magazine. The worst she had to look forward to was the humiliation of meeting him again and apologising for her words; and the best, she thought with a surprising optimism, was her chance to lobby him on Wyatt Mining's reclamation policies or, to be more exact, their non-existence.

'Jo?'

She reluctantly emerged from her thoughts to concentrate on Emily's eager face. 'Yes?'

'Will you come?'

'Oh, yes,' Jo said with a touch of grimness. 'Wild horses couldn't keep me away.'

CHAPTER THREE

ON the first few days of her stay in Conrad Wyatt's home, Jo wished fervently that she'd been more adamant with Emily and more insistent that they not impose on the Wyatts' hospitality. She had never in her life been exposed to more luxury and elegance, and it made her decidedly uncomfortable. Even though she'd known that Conrad, as the head of Wyatt Mining, had to be well-off, she hadn't suspected that his financial resources would be so great. The man who had camped so rustically on the mountainside lived in a home of thick carpets, leather and teak furniture and every modern convenience from a microwave oven in the kitchen to a sauna in the basement.

The house looked nothing like Jo's conception of a ranch, a weatherbeaten building with a barn and acres of rough brush that was based on all the westerns she had ever seen. Instead, she'd found a large, ultra-modern cedar home surrounded by a wide expanse of green lawn and shaded by rows of thickly-leaved poplars. She knew enough about the effect of the dry Alberta climate on grass and shrubbery to appreciate the kind of care such a lawn entailed and the amount of money that must have been spent on the bushes and trees that surrounded the house in such a picturesque fashion.

Despite its urban look, the Wyatt acreage did include barns as Jo had discovered on one of her outdoor excursions, and they were as neat and as orderly as the house in their boundary of white picket fencing. The interiors had freshly-painted stalls, new-mown hay and well-groomed horses whose saddles and bridles gleamed from the application of oil and elbow grease. She had enjoyed the quiet of the barns, the soft nickering sound

39

of the horses and their curious, liquid dark eyes, but she hadn't returned after her first visit. The barns were presided over by a short, bow-legged individual with a broad-brimmed hat and an enormous cigar who went by the handle, Big John Cassidy. From his terse welcome, laconic answers to her questions and the audible mutterings that issued from under his hat, Jo had received the distinct impression that he had a less than warm opinion of strangers in general, Easterners in particular and even more precisely, dang-fool women.

The Wyatt housekeeper was far more cheerful and welcoming. She was a plump, grey-haired woman named Mrs Beattie, and she was obviously delighted to have Jo and Emily under her roof. She didn't seem to mind that Emily required meal trays, and help getting to and from the bathroom, and she even seemed to enjoy the mothering that such care entailed. She consulted with Jo on menus that would tempt Emily's small appetite and made sure that Emily had every comfort she could provide. Between Mrs Beattie and Paul who was also waiting on her hand and foot, Emily could have been spoiled beyond redemption.

But Jo had to admit that, without Paul, she wouldn't have known how to keep up Emily's flagging spirits. Her daily care was onerous. Every task seemed insurmountable, from taking a bath to changing the television channel, and there was almost nothing that she could accomplish on her own. Negotiating the stairs was impossible, and she was confined to her second-storey bedroom unless Paul and Big John carried her downstairs where she could rest on a *chaise-lounge* on the patio. Rather than making her cheerful, these small excursions often made Emily droop listlessly although she tried to conceal her unhappiness behind a quick smile. Paul and Jo soon realised that Emily tired more easily than they had realised and that being downstairs intensified her frustration at being an invalid. She couldn't swim in the kidney-shaped pool, play tennis in the court behind the house or go horseback riding in the fenced corral that was visible from the patio.

Jo found that Emily preferred to sit out on the balcony by her bedroom that overlooked the front of the house, and Paul re-doubled his efforts to keep her amused. Not that the task seemed to strike him as burdensome. He had a large supply of card and board games and when their interest in those palled, he and Emily read plays, taking different parts and dramatic poses. Jo often found them laughing over a comedy and once caught them trying to enact a love scene, not the easiest undertaking with Emily's bulky cast. Paul had squeezed next to her on her lounger and pulled her up to his chest with his left arm while trying to declaim passionately from the script of a melodrama which he held in his right hand.

' "Oh, fair maiden'," he read. ' "Your eyes, blue as the midnight sky and . . ." '

'Afternoon sky,' Emily said, giggling.

'Quiet, fair maiden,' he growled. ' "And your lips that taste of cherry." ' He looked back down at Emily's upturned face. 'Hmmm—perhaps I should test that.'

Only Jo's arrival stopped the ensuing kiss from turning into anything more than a friendly embrace and Paul immediately got off the lounger, but she unhappily recognised in Emily's flushed face and shining eyes all the symptoms of a heavy infatuation. Jo had stayed with them for the rest of the afternoon, but she hated the role of prissy chaperon and she knew Emily resented her presence. Paul was far more successful at making Emily happy than she was and the realisation hurt her more than she liked to admit. Without quite acknowledging her failure, Jo began to take long walks by herself, leaving Emily alone with Paul and desperately trying to keep her mind busy with other occupations.

She spent a great deal of her time walking around Conrad's domain. He wasn't there, and Paul didn't expect to see him for several days. He had flown to the

coast on business while Paul was still in the hospital
and become so tied up with conferences and meetings
that the visit had dragged on for an extra week. Jo
didn't care; in fact, she preferred his absence, but she
couldn't help finding the long hours alone tedious and
boring. She had no money for shopping and any urge
that she had to learn how to ride was dampened by Big
John's obvious misogyny.

The beginning of her explorations took Jo outside.
The Wyatt house stood on a bluff that overlooked the
Bow River, a blue thread of water that meandered
through the vast brown and gold ocean of the prairie to
the green of the foothills and reached the mountains
whose peaks were white even in the height of summer.
Every day the sky was clear, the sun a blazing white
disc against a background of blue. From morning until
night the wind blew, and Jo found its constant motion
astonishing, understanding for the first time stories she
had read of pioneers who had gone insane from its
incessant din. When she walked through the long
grasses, the wind pulled and tugged at her hair,
whipping the black strands back from her head with its
strong, clutching fingers.

There was no escaping the harsh and elemental
nature of the Alberta landscape; no hills to hide the
austere horizon or acres of trees to soften the onslaught
of the wind and shade the viewer from the glittery
brilliance of the sun, and Jo guessed that Conrad had
decorated his house in soothing earth colours with an
eye to softening his environment. The rooms were all
pleasing and muted; the furniture large and comfortable.
Texture and design replaced the need for dramatic
colour. The living room had one mirrored wall that
reflected the mountains through a sliding glass door.
The creamy-beige carpet was not only thick but had a
pattern running through it that reminded Jo of the way
the prairie grasses bent before the wind. Her own room
was spacious and airy, designed in rust and white;
Emily's was in brown and gold.

The master bedroom suite was something of a surprise. Jo had expected everything from a spartan environment to a bachelor's dream pad, but she had not anticipated the walls lined with books, the original paintings or the big, brown leather chair that sat beside the wide bed under its terracotta spread. A Siamese cat was lying on it, its sleek grey body curled, its slanted blue eyes narrowed and watchful as Jo walked around, peering at the titles of books and studying the paintings.

It was a room that was obviously comfortable and very much lived in by a man with a wide range of interests. The titles on the bookshelves ran the gamut from modern fiction to Shakespeare and the styles of paintings were diverse: portraits, landscapes and a still-life. As hard as she tried Jo couldn't fit the absent Conrad into a convenient niche. She had seen the outdoorsman and had guessed at the aggressive, ruthless businessman, but she knew nothing about the man who cultivated the arts and literature and had a taste in decorating that was so close to her own. Jo admired Conrad's house, but its very luxury unnerved her. The Wyatts were from an economic class that far surpassed her own, and Jo was well aware of the way the rich could snub the poor. Paul might be gracious; perhaps he was too young to recognise that the Davidson sisters came, if not from the other side of the tracks, then not far from it, but Jo suspected that Conrad would guess immediately. She knew from bitter experience that others had, and she didn't think that he would prove an exception.

The feeling that Emily's reach had far exceeded her grasp made Jo, already on edge about Conrad's return, even more apprehensive. Her fears made her aloof and cool; she felt safer hiding behind a polite façade and Paul, more than once, had given her a curious glance as if he wondered why Emily had such a peculiar sister. Jo didn't much care what Paul thought of her: Conrad was the man she was going to have to face.

While Jo worried and fretted, Paul and Emily were

eagerly making arrangements for Conrad's return. Paul
and Mrs Beattie had conferred on a menu for dinner
that night, and although Jo was not included in the
planning, she knew that great plans were afoot for a
gourmet meal. Emily wanted to join them for dinner
and insisted that she be bathed and changed into
regular clothes. Because her full-leg cast required that
Emily have a sponge bath in bed, it took Jo most of the
afternoon to help her get ready. But when they were
done, she saw that the effort had been worthwhile.

She couldn't blame Emily for being sick to death of
wearing a nightgown and robe, and she looked much
less the invalid in a blue-sprigged cotton blouse and
denim skirt. Jo had washed her long blonde hair and
plaited it into a French braid on the back of her head.
Emily always looked older when her hair was pulled
back from her slender face, and a touch of make-up on
her blue eyes made them appear even wider. Paul and
Big John carried her down the stairs, wrists and hands
clasped together into a seat while Emily put an arm
around each man's shoulder. They were just settling her
into the cushions on the living room couch when a deep
voice spoke in the living room doorway.

'Where's the welcome for the returning warrior?'

Conrad was leaning nonchalantly against the door
jamb, his level grey eyes appraising each of them one by
one and then coming to rest on Jo, who discovered that
a lump had grown in her throat and that her heart was
beating in a strange rapid fashion. Her memory of
Conrad paled next to the reality, just as the image of
the blue-jeaned camper faded next to that of the
executive. He was dressed in a pale grey suit, white shirt
and diagonally-striped blue and silver tie. The jacket
had been tailored to emphasise the width of his
shoulders and was unbuttoned to reveal a flat abdomen
tapering to narrow hips. He was tired; Jo could see the
fatigue that marked the skin around his eyes, but he
was still, by far, one of the most good-looking men she
had ever seen. Movie-star good looks: thick, waving

blond hair, bronzed skin over high cheekbones and a dark-gold moustache that framed the strong curve of his mouth.

Jo felt at a terrible disadvantage. She was still in bare feet; her faded jeans were rolled up unevenly on her calves; and her skimpy T-shirt was damp from Emily's bath. Not to mention the fact that she wasn't wearing a speck of make-up and her black hair was in a tangle around her head. It was a relief when the others went to greet Conrad, blocking him from her view. Her grip loosened on the back of the couch and her breath, unconsciously held in during his appraisal, released in a soft sigh.

After Mrs Beattie, Big John and Paul had greeted him, Conrad walked towards the couch and kneeled down before Emily. 'So this is Emily,' he said gently. 'How's the ankle?'

She gave him a shy smile. 'It's getting better.'

'Have Paul and Mrs Beattie been looking after you properly?'

As Emily nodded, Paul came closer. 'We've been devoted slaves, Con, if you really want to know the truth. And she's a slave-driver, too. I've been chained to the Monopoly set for hours at a time.'

'Paul!' Emily protested, but Conrad just smiled, the laughter lines crinkling around his amused eyes.

'I wouldn't mind a game of Monopoly,' he said.

'Don't agree, Emily,' Paul interjected. 'He cheats.'

Emily gave Paul a teasing look. 'I'd wondered where you got it from.'

'Me?' Paul exclaimed heatedly. 'I don't cheat; I'm as honest as the day is long.'

'And since I've already known you for more than twenty-four hours, it's been downhill ever since,' Emily replied severely.

The banter between Paul and Emily faded into the background as Conrad stood up and faced Jo. They stared at each other for a long minute, both unsmiling as if they were enemies and judging hostile terrain. Jo didn't like what she saw—a man who could charm her sister with a few words, who had the power to make her feel like a fool and whose eyes even now held a hint of mockery at her discomfiture.

'We meet again,' Conrad murmured.

Jo hated the flush that rose to her cheeks. With one brief phrase, Conrad had managed to remind her of all the intimate and unpleasant details of their previous meeting. She was just trying to think of a suitable response when Paul broke in:

'Hey, I didn't know you two were acquainted.'

Conrad turned to his nephew. 'Didn't Miss Davidson tell you that our campsites were within calling distance?'

Now both Emily and Paul were looking at her. 'You never mentioned it, Jo,' Emily said in confusion.

'It . . . skipped my mind,' Jo stammered slightly.

'It seems you have a short memory, Miss Davidson,' Conrad said silkily.

Jo's amber eyes narrowed. 'It's getting longer by the minute, Mr Wyatt,' she said, her tone warning him that she had neither forgotten nor forgiven him for concealing his identity and conniving with Paul to bring Emily to the ranch.

'Hey,' Paul protested, stepping innocently into the line of battle, 'there's no need to be so formal. Con, this is Jo. Jo, this my uncle, Conrad. We're all friends, right?'

'Yes,' said Jo, flashing Conrad a small, grim smile before turning to Paul. 'We're all friends.'

Jo was hesitant to describe her 'friendly' relationship with Conrad as warfare, but the fact that it was silent was just as unnerving as if it had been a screaming and yelling match. Her determination to convert Conrad to an environmentalist point of view never got off the ground. During the weekend that followed his return, they barely spoke to one another except in polite conversation at the dinner table. All the charm that

Conrad possessed was turned on to Emily, who blossomed even further under the attention of two attractive men. Paul continued his daily servitude and Conrad expressed a great interest in the responsibilities of a kindergarten teacher.

Jo was far less susceptible to the combined Wyatt charm than her sister, and she watched with a great deal of suspicion the efforts both men made to make Emily happy and cheerful. She still believed that Paul was having a summer dalliance before heading back to university in September, and she could see no future in a trans-state relationship. Emily had to return to New York and take up her teaching post. Yet, it was obvious that she was falling further in love with Paul every day, and Jo began to steel herself for the task of picking up all the shattered pieces of Emily's hopes when the flirtation ended, as it inevitably would, on the rocks.

It angered her that Conrad turned a blind eye towards his nephew's irresponsible behaviour when he could see what a trusting soul Emily was. Not that she had really thought he would worry about her sister, but she was surprised and disturbed that he didn't expect more from Paul whom he'd had under his care for fifteen formative years. Didn't he care that Paul was taking a young woman's vulnerability and fashioning it into an adoration that he didn't reciprocate? She thought it was immoral to be so careless of another's happiness, and she'd had hopes that Conrad would restrain Paul's behaviour, but when he did nothing of the kind, Jo could only come to the conclusion that uncle and nephew were two of a kind, adept at ensnaring hearts and then discarding them like used toys.

There was certainly evidence in the house that Conrad had a number of women friends. Jo had found several pairs of pantyhose that were decidedly not Mrs Beattie's size, in one of the drawers in her dresser; two bestsellers that Jo had read during the past week from the bookshelf in his bedroom had been given to Conrad with love from a certain Marion; and during Conrad's absence he had received several letters with a return address in Manhattan that were mauve in colour, scented with lavender and written in a flowing female hand. Jo wasn't naïve enough to think that a man of Conrad's age and good-looks existed without women, but his single state suggested that he didn't take them seriously either, a suspicion that was confirmed on the morning she helped Mrs Beattie make apple pies for Sunday dinner.

The housekeeper, she had found, was an affable person who liked to talk. Jo had already been acquainted with all the facts of her life; the farm she grew up on in the little town of nearby Drumheller; her husband's early heart attack; the cute things that her grandchildren said; and how much she enjoyed working for Conrad Wyatt. As an employer, it seemed that Conrad reached a level of unbelievable perfection. Jo was forced to listen to several long monologues about Conrad's virtues; his neatness, his flair for organisation, his down-to-earth manner, his easy-going temperament.

'Never complains,' Mrs Beattie said as she rolled a pastry crust. 'Not even when the house is crowded with guests.'

'Conrad entertains a lot?' Jo asked as she deftly peeled a apple.

'Whenever he's here. He does a lot of travelling, you know. Although I don't think it's completely necessary.'

'Not necessary?'

'He's got nothing to keep him at home.' Mrs Beattie made a scolding sound with her tongue. 'No family ties.'

Jo began to slice an apple with sharp little motions. 'He has Paul,' she said.

Mrs Beattie shook her head as she wiped her hands on the voluminous apron that wrapped her plump frame. 'He's lonely. It's not everybody that can see past the smiles to the man beneath. But I've been around long enough to know.'

'Lonely?' Jo looked up in astonishment. 'I would think he had plenty of . . . girl friends.'

Mrs Beattie brushed the assorted females aside with a wave of her hand. 'They come and go; it doesn't mean a thing.'

There was a silence while Jo picked up another apple and Mrs Beattie resumed rolling out the dough. Jo was digesting her words and finding them almost unpalatable. She couldn't see that Conrad was lonely. He had the ranch, Paul, his business and enough women to satisfy his desires. Saying that he was lonely was as ridiculous as Emily's assertion that Jo felt the same way. Her disbelief must have shown on her face because Mrs Beattie proceeded to outline all the reasons why she thought Conrad wanted a wife.

'Mr Conrad needs a family and children. It's not natural for him to go through life, running from pillar to post, with no roots. Of course, he's had to sow his wild oats, but he's thirty-seven now and through that stage. He might not realise exactly what he needs yet, but every once in a while he gets quiet and sort of melancholy. You can tell then that something's missing.'

Jo remembered the night she had spent in Conrad's tent and had her own opinions about Conrad's wild oats. 'He looks content to me,' she said with a shrug.

But Mrs Beattie was adamant. 'He needs a woman, that's what I say.' She slapped the crust into the pie plate with determination. 'And when he finds the right one, he won't let her go. I know Mr Conrad, that's the way he is.'

Later that evening, as Jo prepared for bed, she found Mrs Beattie's words running through her mind. All through that Sunday afternoon and dinner, she'd surreptitiously kept her eye on Conrad to see if his behaviour bore out Mrs Beattie's opinions. She couldn't see that he was lonely or melancholy at all. He'd spent the afternoon with Big John, riding around the periphery of the ranch, checking on fences. For an hour before dinner, he had read the Sunday papers and made light conversation with Emily. During dinner he and Paul had casually discussed the local political scene, and when the meal was over he had excused himself, claiming a vast amount of paperwork for the next day's meeting of his Board of Directors. The most peaceful day of his week had been chockful of activity, and Jo couldn't see any evidence that Conrad was missing anything except a chance to put his feet up and relax.

Mrs Beattie's words merely enforced Jo's contention that Conrad was quite self-sufficient and not particularly interested in complicating his life by adding a wife as a permanent fixture. Bachelorhood seemed to suit him and it was obvious that he was forming Paul in the same mould. She wondered why he had invited Emily and herself to stay at his ranch and then came to the conclusion that Paul had persuaded him to issue the invitation. He had virtually ignored her for the whole weekend, and she no longer thought that he had any interest in obtaining her apology, talking to her about their mutual interest in mining or even making the sexual overture she'd been waiting for. As far as Jo was concerned, Conrad barely knew she existed.

Which was all to the good, she told herself that night as she sat before the mirror on her dresser and began to brush her hair. She preferred their cold, polite exchanges to anything more heated. She'd decided long ago that their were other mining magnates besides Conrad Wyatt to interview and, if they weren't available, she would be able to write her article anyway. Her own research and the visual impact of seeing the erosion of the mountains for herself was inspiration enough.

And if she felt any chagrin that Conrad preferred to act as if she weren't there, Jo didn't admit it to herself. She sat before the mirror on her dresser that Sunday evening and brushed her hair with long, vigorous strokes, counting each one and aiming towards one hundred. She'd had enough experience with men to know that there was sexual tension in the air. She and Conrad had passed one another several times in a hallway or on the stairs and had mutually pressed closer to the walls so that their bodies wouldn't touch. She had been aloof; he had been cold, neither acknowledging the electricity generated when their eyes briefly met.

'Twenty-five,' Jo said softly, her hair crackling under the bristles of the brush. 'Twenty-six.' Still, she knew that the feeling Conrad aroused in her, that sudden and unexpected visceral interest in a man, was perhaps a true sign that she had got over Douglas and that her senses were coming alive after a long bout of hibernation. As Emily had said, Jo hadn't dated for almost three years or considered any man more than as an acquaintance. It had been an asexual and abnormal existence; Jo was aware of that, but she had welcomed it, burying herself ever deeper into her work and her family. She distrusted this renewal of sensation, knowing that if she weren't careful it could be dangerous and hurtful like the opening of a safely locked Pandora's box of emotions.

Jo sighed as she made her thirtieth stroke. Conrad was so evidently the wrong man in the wrong place at the wrong time, and she reflected on the perversity of attraction. Like the time and tides, it was uncontrollable, inexorable and relentless in its momentum. She had no choice but to endure its more unpleasant aspects, the sudden stopping of her heart at the sight of blond hair and broad shoulders and the quickened intake of her breath when a pair of grey eyes glanced in her direction. She had only three weeks left of her stay in Calgary, and surely . . .

There was a quick, light rapping at her door and Jo, thinking it must be Mrs Beattie with the extra towels she had mentioned earlier, called out a welcome. She didn't notice who actually entered until she happened to glance upwards into the mirror and saw Conrad leaning against the closed door, tall and lean in a black shirt and jeans.

A sudden constriction in her throat almost made it impossible for Jo to speak. 'What . . . do you want?' she stammered, turning in her chair.

'To talk to you,' he said.

'I'm not dressed,' she said breathlessly.

Conrad glanced at the demure neckline of her long blue nightgown and gave a lazy smile. 'I've seen more flesh on a beach.'

Jo relinquished any hope she had of getting rid of Conrad. 'What do you want to talk about?'

He uncoiled himself from the door and sat down in a chair by Jo's bed, crossing his arms over his broad chest and putting his stockinged feet up on the spread. 'For a woman with the sharpest tongue west of the Mississippi, you've been strangely subdued all weekend.'

'I've never been a chatty type.'

'Nor sociable?'

Jo gave him a levelled amber look. 'I'm uncomfortable here,' she said coldly. 'I didn't want to come in the first place. I'm sure you know that.'

'Is that why Emily keeps apologising for you?'

Jo blinked in astonishment. 'Emily apologises for me?'

'She keeps assuring us that you're not at all the way you seem, and that you're so used to working hard that you don't know how to relax. She . . .'

'I . . . I can't believe Emily said that.'

Conrad shrugged. 'Straight from the horse's mouth.'

Jo quickly looked down at the floor where the hem of her nightgown brushed the ankles of her bare feet. She was horrified that Emily had felt the need to apologise for her behaviour. It had never occurred to Jo that Emily might feel ashamed by what she said or the way she acted, and she cringed at the thought of her kid sister defending her before strangers.

She gritted her teeth and looked up at Conrad. 'I'm the one who should be apologising . . . for the way I spoke to you about Wyatt Mining.'

' "The ruthless plunderer",' Conrad quoted with a grin. 'I liked that; it had a swashbuckling sound.'

'I wouldn't be proud of it,' Jo said coldly.

'No, you wouldn't,' he said dryly, 'but then you're into changing the world from a lofty position of righteousness.'

'I don't have to defend land reclamation,' Jo retorted. 'Any fool can see that your company is destroying the Rockies.'

'And any fool can make statements without the least bit of knowledge.'

'I know about coal reclamation!'

'But nothing about running a mine,' he said sarcastically. 'I've noticed how poorly informed you and your crusading friends generally are.'

Jo was caught for a moment. Conrad had quite accurately pointed out one of her weaknesses. She didn't know the first thing about the economics of running any business, much less a mine. Her ignorance made her vulnerable, and Jo had often thought that she should take a quick immersion course in business management, but she had never been able to find the time. Still, she wasn't the sort to yield an advantage. 'The least you could do,' she said pointedly, 'is apologise for concealing your identity.'

Conrad slanted one golden eyebrow. 'Is that what's bothering you?'

'It was devious,' Jo began, 'and . . .'

'Here, I thought you were upset about the night we spent together,' he said, his eyes gleaming grey through their golden lashes.

Jo shrugged indifferently. 'Why should I be?'

'Most of the women I know would have found it amusing.'

'I guess I'm different from your female acquaintances,' she retorted.

'You know something, New York, I really can't figure why you're here.'

'Because of Emily.'

'You're not your sister's keeper,' he retorted.

'She needs protection.'

'Oh, I don't know,' Conrad drawled. 'Emily strikes me as the type to take care of herself.'

'I don't think so,' she said, her eyes a cold amber. It was audacious of Conrad to assume that he knew her sister far better than she did. He'd known Emily for a weekend; Jo remembered the day her sister learned how to walk.

Conrad's cheekbones gleamed bronze in the beam of a nearby lamp. 'You don't trust Paul.'

'I . . . no, I don't.'

'Your sister is a grown woman.'

'She's a babe in the woods as far as men are concerned.'

'And you, of course, have more experience,' he said softly.

Jo clenched her teeth together. 'Much more.'

'A bad love affair?'

Jo didn't deign to answer. 'Look,' she said, aiming for an even tone. 'Why not call it quits. I'm here for certain reasons whether I like it or not.'

Conrad leaned even farther back in the chair. 'I have a theory about people, New York—that no one acts without self-interest being paramount.'

'What a cynical view!' Jo said, turning back to the mirror and beginning to brush her hair again, determined to show Conrad that his philosophical leanings were not of interest to her.

'I don't think I'm cynical—merely pragmatic. Most people do what they want to do even if they won't admit it to themselves.'

Jo glared at his image in the mirror as she pulled the brush through the long thick strands of her hair. 'Are you implying that I want to be here, Emily or not?'

'You're quick on the draw.'

'Well, you're wrong. Wild horses couldn't have dragged me here if it hadn't been for Emily. She needs medical care and supervision and . . .'

Conrad moved so quickly and quietly that his presence behind her caught Jo unawares. He stood close to her back and their eyes met in the mirror, amber and grey, gold and silver, mingling in the reflection and held to one another in magnetic attraction. Jo found that she could hardly breathe and unconsciously the tips of her breasts hardened beneath the thin fabric of her nightgown where the material, pulled taut by the arm she had lifted to her head, revealed their outline and form.

The grey eyes flicked down and then met Jo's gaze again as Conrad reached out slowly, reluctantly as if his hand were heavily weighted, and tangled his fingers in her black hair, tightening them convulsively among its strands. 'Why did you come here, New York?'

'I told you—because of Emily,' she replied.

Jo saw his mouth harden. 'That's not the truth.'

'It is!'

'Emily is merely your excuse.'

'I don't know what you're talking about,' she said breathlessly. She tried to move, but his hand was against her scalp, his grip so secure on her hair that she couldn't even shift her head to look away.

'You wanted to come here; you wanted to see me again.'

'No!'

'Do you deny that we share a mutual attraction for one another?' he questioned.

'Yes!'

'You're a liar, and a damn bad one, at that.' His fingers moved through her hair, curving down the back of her head and resting on the sensitive nape of her neck. Jo discovered that she couldn't have moved if she had wanted to; she was mesmerised by his eyes; a darkened grey, watching and slightly amused.

Her voice was shaky. 'I think you'd better leave.'

The warm fingers massaged her neck. 'From the moment I saw you in the hospital,' he said softly, 'I decided that I wanted you.'

'This is ridiculous,' she breathed. 'You didn't even know me; we were strangers, we . . .'

'I'm a simple man, New York—not one of those complicated Easterners that has to cover up his wants and desires with a lot of fancy jargon and pretty words. This is a very elemental country out here; you'll see that for yourself. Survival is a question of cutting through the false veneer of civilisation and discovering what lies below. Those who have failed have crept back to their cities with their tails between their legs.'

Jo had regained some composure throughout his speech. 'Aren't you just protesting a bit much?' she asked sarcastically. 'I would call electricity, running water and a microwave oven extremely civilised.'

'Come out with me on to the prairie, face the adversity of the wind and the sun and find out who you really are.'

'I know who I am.'

'No,' he said, his voice low, 'I don't think you do at all.'

Jo thought he was going to lean down and kiss her neck and she stiffened in anticipation of his touch. But Conrad did nothing of the sort. He merely let go of her hair, his fingers drifting along her shoulder, their warmth heating her through the thin fabric of her gown. He smiled at her lazily and with a knowing amusement that made a rush of pink rise to her cheeks until her eyes fell from the intensity of his gaze.

'You're a beautiful woman, New York,' he said. 'Too bad you fight it so hard.' And with that, he was gone, leaving Jo frozen on her chair, staring at the reflection of the door in the mirror as if his long back with its broad shoulders had been imprinted on the wood panels for all time.

She still felt his fingers pulling on her hair; his hand against her skin. Conrad was unlike any man she had ever met. He was direct, forceful and unafraid to speak what he thought. Without hesitation he had reduced their conflict to its most basic element: that unspoken attraction that lay between them like a dark, uncharted territory. Jo may have denied its existence to the outside world but she couldn't resist an enemy that lay within her own soul. She had felt a rush of desire, hot and intense, when Conrad had held her gaze in the smoky grey of his eyes and then twisted her hair in his lean fingers. And like a river that has been dammed too long, it had swept away her defences, those emotional barricades she had so carefully erected in the past, and flowed unhindered into every fibre and sinew of her being.

CHAPTER FOUR

ODDLY enough, Jo dreamed about Douglas Bannock that night. In her dream, he had come to Calgary and met her in the long prairie grass behind the Wyatt house. She wore a long denim skirt and a frilly Mexican blouse, her feet bare against the tough blades. He rode up to her on a horse, a black fierce horse with a flowing mane that made Jo step back and cringe in fear. Douglas spoke to her but she couldn't hear the words; the prairie wind took them out of his mouth and swept them past her so that they made a sound like a tape or record being run too quickly. She only knew that he was beckoning to her to climb on, but she was far too afraid of both the horse and the man and she began to run from him, tripping over her skirt and falling against the dry earth, the sun beating down all the while on her bare head, the hot wind tugging at her hair, until she thought she might faint. I should have worn my sombrero, Jo thought frantically to herself in the dream, although in real life she didn't own a sombrero, a denim skirt or a blouse that slipped down over one shoulder.

The horse came, inching towards her despite its great strength, and she realised that time had now slowed down. She waited in an agony of suspense and fear. The horse's legs beat thunderously against the ground like black pillars, making the earth shudder, and she threw her arm over her eyes to shield her against the destructive force of its hooves. But when nothing happened she took her arm down and stared up at the figure on the horse and saw that it was no longer Douglas but Conrad who held the black stallion in check, the reins held tautly to his chest, the brim of his stetson low over his eyes, his mouth stretched into a grin beneath the golden moustache. He laughed, a booming sound that filled her ears, hurting them, beating against them in an incessant pattern, like rain, falling, dropping on . . .

Jo woke to find that the laughter was real, right outside the door to her bedroom. She blinked into the wide swathe of intense sunshine that came through the window curtains and fell across her shoulder and face in a warm embrace. A door banged, there was a muffled curse and then Emily's giggle was added to Conrad's laughter.

'Damn it,' Paul said. 'That door has some nerve, smashing into my shin that way.'

'Try sweet talk,' Conrad said. 'Even a door needs attention.'

There was a shuffling sound and then Paul said, 'Okay, Emily, up you go and don't wiggle.'

'If you'd get your hand lower . . .'

'Service,' Paul complained. 'All this lady wants is full-time service. I tell you, Em, you're going to miss this cast when it goes.'

'Are you kidding?'

Conrad's deep voice. 'How often do you get two willing slaves to wait on you hand and, well, foot.'

'Ugh,' Emily commented on his joke.

'Thank God, Emily has enough courage to tell you what she really thinks of your lousy puns, Con. The rest of us have been forced to suffer in silence.'

'Paul has a poor sense of humour,' Conrad informed Emily, 'and it doesn't come from my side of the family.'

'He can be sour,' Emily agreed.

'Hey,' Paul protested as the voices faded down the corridor. 'What did I do to deserve that?'

Jo sat up in bed, pushed away the tangle of hair from her forehead and brought her knees up to her chest, pulling her nightgown down to her toes and wrapping her arms around her knees. As the voices receded, the memory of her dream grew stronger and Jo shivered a little in its aftermath. She had an uneasy feeling of danger and a sensation of forces moving beyond her control. She was neither skilled enough in introspection or versed enough in the meaning of dreams, to understand that the fierce horse symbolised her own sexuality, in all its strength and force, and that its rider, the man who controlled and manipulated that sensuality, represented a frightening and dominating power over her. She only knew that she couldn't quite shake the dream's effects, and that it was only with the greatest effort afterwards that she was able to force away the image of Conrad laughing down at her, his teeth strong and white in the hot Alberta sun, whenever his name was mentioned, even in passing.

That afternoon Paul drove Emily and Jo into downtown Calgary where the orthopaedics specialist, recommended by the Pincher Creek doctor, had his office. Emily's ankle was pronounced to be coming along as well as could be expected, and the doctor promised her that he'd change her cast to something smaller and more manageable on her next visit. The news cheered Emily immensely, and she chattered and laughed as Paul drove them through the city, pointing out the Indians who had grown up on reservations on the outskirts of Calgary, the tall, revolving Husky Tower whose multi-faceted glass enclosure offered a panoramic view of the mountains to the west, and the store windows displaying boots of carved and studded leather, shirts with hand embroidered yokes and full-brimmed hats, some decorated with feathers and colourful bands.

'Now I know why you grew up wanting to be a cowboy,' Emily said to Paul.

He negotiated the car past a truck and said, 'My biggest dream was to wear a six-shooter and act like Wyatt Earp. In fact, I was convinced that the sheriff and I were relatives of some sort because we shared the same name. Imagine my ten-year-old dismay when Uncle Con informed me, in the most callous fashion I might add, that not only wasn't Wyatt my great-great grandfather, but that my ancestors came from such citified places as Toronto and Seattle.'

'Poor Paul,' Emily murmured, throwing him a laughing glance from between her lashes.

'Con had a way of bursting my bubbles,' Paul went on in a good-natured way. 'First there was Santa Claus and then the Easter bunny. He really knew how to hurt a guy.'

Jo, suddenly curious despite her efforts not to think about Conrad at all, leaned forward from her seat in the back of the car. 'How long have you lived with Conrad, Paul?'

'Since I was seven.'

'Where are your parents?'

'I couldn't give you my father's precise location,' Paul said easily. 'It seems that he wasn't the staying kind. He lit out after I was born and hasn't been seen since.'

'And your mother? Is she Conrad's sister?'

This time Paul's voice held a slim edge of bitterness and Jo saw Emily put one hand over his on the wheel as he spoke. 'Half-sister and a lady who prefers marriage to children. She's on her fourth husband and spends her time in Europe jetsetting from one exotic locale to another. I cramped her style so she handed me over to Conrad. That's why I use the Wyatt name.'

'Oh, I . . .' What could one say in response to such news? 'Our parents are divorced, too.'

'So Emily tells me.'

Emily turned her head towards Jo. 'Paul and I have a lot in common—broken bones . . .'

'I'm almost healed.' Paul jiggled his still-bandaged elbow up and down.

'Divorced parents,' Emily went on, 'Monopoly, Scrabble, old plays, the colour blue, sheepdogs, tacos . . .'

'Don't forget—chocolate milkshakes, movies . . .'

'Not horror films though.'

'Not horror films,' Paul acquiesced, 'gin rummy, mystery novels, blondes . . .'

'Paul!' Emily said in mock-horror. 'I like brunettes.' And they grinned at one another, Emily's blonde head close to Paul's dark one, effectively cutting Jo out of their circle and forcing her to sit back in her seat and stare determinedly out of the window as the suburbs of Calgary sped by. She knew that they didn't mean to push her away but they had a fault common to new lovers around the world—they saw only each other to the exclusion of everyone and anything else.

The thought of Emily and Paul's deepening intimacy made Jo feel glum, miserable and lonely for several days afterwards. She saw no way of putting a halt to the relationship short of kidnapping Emily and taking her away from the Wyatt house. She knew that she was powerless to act until Emily's cast was changed and they could manage the long ride back to New York in the car together. Jo's only consolation lay in her conviction that Emily and Paul's relationship had not evolved in physical terms. To put it bluntly, Jo didn't think that they were sleeping together, which meant that the inevitable break would be much easier to bear when it came. Jo knew how devastated she had felt when Douglas had walked out of her life and she didn't want Emily to suffer in kind.

Still, she couldn't bear to stay around Paul and Emily. Their happiness set her on edge and, in an attempt to escape her thoughts, she spent most of her time in the den, her feet up on a red leather ottoman, her nose buried in a thriller. She found herself turning pages she hadn't read and trying to follow the stories of characters that she couldn't keep track of. Her mind kept straying in odd directions and she found her eyes wandering off to the window where she could see the line of mountains, grey and peaked against the incredible blue of the sky. In the distance, they looked one-dimensional; immense cardboard cutouts placed on the earth by the hand of a giant. From where she sat, they gave no inkling of the rages of weather and elements that existed on their peaks; they sat in a seemingly peaceful solitude, arranged to grace the horizon in a wide, curving row.

Conrad's words of the night he had come into her room often came into her mind—that this was an elemental country that made the weak turn tail, where the survival meant learning what lay beneath the surface of politeness and gentility. He hadn't minced words; he had told her what he thought of her, and Jo had known that there was some truth in what he had said. She *had* hidden her heart and her emotions beneath a hard veneer. She had never denied it to herself, but she saw survival in different terms from Conrad. She wouldn't last for a second if she let her mask down and allowed her vulnerabilities to show. Douglas had already shown her just how malleable and gullible she could be when her barrier was down and the real Jo lay exposed to the world. It was dangerous to be that innocent and naïve.

No, Jo decided on the Friday afternoon following her trip into Calgary with Emily and Paul, she preferred to see her façade as a shield of experience. It allowed her to hide her desire and to treat Conrad as if he were nothing more than an acquaintance. She had no intention of revealing herself to a man whose interest in her was purely sexual, whose admitted first thought on seeing her was to get her into bed. She simply wasn't the kind of woman who could engage in sex merely for its physical pleasures, and she had no idea how much companionship she required before she did sleep with a man. She had certainly trusted Douglas and had known of him long before . . .

'So there you are.' Conrad was leaning against the doorjamb, his grey suit jacket open, the knot in his tie undone and his hair tousled as if the wind had whipped through it.

'I've been reading.'

'Anything good?'

Jo held the book up so he could see its title. 'Murder and mystery.'

He raised an eyebrow. 'Not bad for a quiet afternoon.'

'Well, Paul and Emily were busy and . . .'

'I know—another championship game of Scrabble. They've reduced the world to one Q, one Z, one J and fourteen E's.'

Jo couldn't help returning his smile. 'Maybe life's easier that way.'

He shrugged wearily. 'Maybe.'

'You've had a hard day?' she asked, knowing the long hours Conrad had been working. She hadn't seen much of him; he'd either been in his office or behind the closed door of his den.

He ran his fingers through his hair in a tired gesture. 'Fighting corporate alligators and keeping one step ahead of the regulatory commissions requires more energy some days than I can accumulate in a week. Maybe I'll go back to riding the range—that's the way I intended to live my life about fifteen years ago.'

'And?'

'And the world interfered. My father had a heart attack and took an early retirement leaving me with the family firm. I went from being a foot-loose and fancy-free cowboy to corporate executive in one swoop of a lawyer's pen.'

'You weren't really a cowboy,' she protested.

Conrad gave her a grin. 'Just one at heart. I was getting a business degree in real life.'

Jo couldn't restrain herself. 'You said you were pragmatic.'

He gave her a level grey look. 'Yes, I did, didn't I?'

The sudden silence between them was interrupted by Mrs Beattie, who came bustling along the hallway in search of Conrad. 'Will there be two or three for dinner then?' she asked him, stopping in the doorway, her full bosom still panting from the exertion of climbing the stairs.

'Two—Jo's going with me.'

Jo sat up in surprise as Mrs Beattie beamed at her. 'It'll give you a taste of our western hospitality. The Beauchamps always have a terrific spread, I hear.'

'And good steak,' Conrad added.

'Their own, isn't that right, Mr Conrad?'

'Prime and right off their own land.'

'Well, have a good time then.' And Mrs Beattie was gone in a flurry of apron and a wafting scent of lavender perfume.

'Where exactly am I going?' Jo asked sarcastically when she was sure Mrs Beattie was out of hearing.

'To a western-style barbecue.'

'Isn't it odd that I don't remember receiving an invitation?'

Conrad gave her a lazy grin. 'Or agreeing to go?'

Jo firmly put down her book. 'I didn't and I would prefer to stay . . .'

'The party will be crawling with environmentalists. I thought you'd fit right in.'

'You mean . . .?'

'I mean you'll be surrounded by kindred souls. Frank Beauchamp owns Alberta Resource and Mining and he's trying to work out some compromise legislation with the environmentalist lobby. Consider the barbecue as half-business, half-pleasure.'

Put in that framework, Jo didn't see how she could refuse. There was always more strength in numbers and she had visions of adding her small but vocal group of environmentalists to the Canadian one. 'I'd love to go,' she said, giving Conrad a gracious smile.

'Somehow,' he said dryly, 'I knew you would.'

The barbecue was going full swing when they arrived, the patio and grounds surrounding the Beauchamps' vast stone house covered with guests chatting, waiters carrying trays and a huge cooking area where young men dressed in white aprons and chefs' hats tended to thick slabs of steak that were being grilled on open fires. Jo, who was accustomed to the occasional back-yard barbecue where everyone brought a pot-luck casserole and the host supplied the sirloin and beer, was a bit overwhelmed by the scene. She was only thankful that the guests, both male and female, were wearing casual western-style clothes, jeans, jean skirts, yoked shirts and the occasional colourful bandana. Jo had been worried that her one non-hiking outfit be out of place, but she saw immediately that she'd fit right in. She wore a simple A-line skirt of navy cotton, a white blouse with a square neckline and a pair of leather sandals, leaving her slender, tanned legs bare. Her only concession to elegance was that she had pulled her hair into a smooth chignon at her neck and made up her face more than usual. Her eyes were highlighted by skilfully applied cream and bronze shadow, her cheekbones outlined by a faint colouring of rouge and her lips softened into glowing peach.

Conrad had changed into tan slacks and a royal-blue pullover that was open in a V half-way down his chest. His bared flesh with its mat of dark-gold hair had a way of making Jo feel distinctly uncomfortable and she had made it a habit from the moment she had got into the car not to look directly at him. His blatant statement of sexual desire had made her all too aware of him as a physical being, and it had taken all of her efforts of concentration to focus on their conversation without being mesmerised by the sight of his lean hands on the wheel or the way his tan slacks stretched across the muscles of his thigh.

And her desire to avoid being close or intimate with Conrad was one of the reasons why, when she caught sight of a face that she knew among the crowd milling on the Beauchamps' patio, her enthusiasm was a bit more exuberant than the occasion warranted.

'Roddy Moore? I don't believe it!'

The man turned, his familiar dark curls making an untidy fringe across his forehead. 'Jo! Long time, no see. What are you doing here?'

'Ah . . .' she sought for the right word as Roddy pulled her into his arms and gave her a hearty kiss on the cheek.

'Visiting,' Conrad said, and Roddy let go of her, although he kept her hand in his.

'How did you come to know the Wyatts?'

'It was . . .' Jo began.

'Accidental,' Conrad finished for her, his grey eyes cool as they took in Jo's flushed face and Roddy's grip on her hand.

'We're old school buddies, aren't we, Jo?' Roddy didn't wait for her answer but perused her face, his round blue eyes approving. 'Hey, you look terrific, kid! The last time I saw you was about four years ago, wasn't it? You were buried in your books and I had decided to head out West after finishing my degree.'

'And that's how you ended up in Calgary?'

Roddy gave her a broad grin which split his square face and turned his eyes into half-moons. He had hardly changed from the days when he and Jo had shared some courses. He was still short, a bit on the plump side and gregarious. 'That's too long a tale for a party,' he said. 'You should come and meet some of the folks.'

'Jo wants to talk to the environmentalists,' Conrad said. 'That's more your bag than mine, Moore.'

Roddy gave Jo a wink. 'Wyatt and Beauchamp are the head of the rape and pillage crowd. We plan on making their lives miserable.'

'Rape and pillage?'

Roddy gave a roar of laughter at Jo's expression. 'The earth, baby, the earth.'

By the time Roddy had finished with her, Jo knew all the important players in the mining industry in Alberta. Roddy, who served as a liaison between government agencies, the mining industry and environmentalist groups, had a back-slapping or hand-shaking relationship with everyone who counted, and Jo could see that the Roddy she had known who had an unquenchable enthusiasm for fraternities, beer parties and football games was ideally suited to his job. He had merely graduated, in a sense, into a wider arena and a larger social network. He led her from group to group, made the introductions and then as they moved away, would give Jo a humorous and slightly malicious footnote on who was who. 'A first-class bastard,' he said of one man. 'Three-quarters wimp and one-quarter bluster,' he said of another. He finally left her with several men from the Alberta Conservation Society, and Jo spent most of the cocktail hour exchanging notes and ideas. It wasn't until she felt a hand on her elbow and turned to find Conrad standing beside her that Jo remembered that she was at a party.

'I think it's time she met the host,' Conrad said smoothly as he pulled Jo out from the group, and she gave him a small, shamed smile.

'Sorry, but I got involved.'

'Learn anything new?'

'It was very interesting,' she began with enthusiasm, but Conrad put up a desisting hand. 'Business later,' he said, 'Now, we're going to aim for pleasure.'

She had, Jo realised, as Conrad introduced her to his friends, forgotten as usual that the men she dealt with in her profession came with wives. Roddy's 'bastard' had a sweet-looking wife with a gentle voice. The 'wimp' was, surprisingly, married to one of the most elegant-looking women at the party. They all seemed to be friends of Conrad's, but the closest were obviously the Beauchamps, a couple in their mid-forties who were dressed in jeans, matching bright red shirts and identical paisley red and blue bandanas. Frank was a big, genial man with a retreating hairline and a comfortable-looking paunch that was presently covered by a large chef's apron; his wife Diane was petite, vivacious, with blonde, short curls and a deep affection for Conrad.

She gave him a big hug and then winked at Jo. 'It must take a houseguest to blast Conrad out of his house,' she said. 'We haven't seen him for weeks.'

'I see Frank almost every day.'

'Pooh,' she said. 'That doesn't count.'

'That's my marriage in a nutshell,' Frank moaned. 'I haven't counted for years.'

Conrad gave Diane a reproving look. 'You're neglecting him.'

'Nonsense,' she said with asperity. 'He's too big to neglect and too noisy to ignore.' She turned a deaf ear to Frank's groan of protest. 'I'm going to monopolise Jo here for a while and leave you two men to suffer together.'

Conrad raised a blond eyebrow in Frank's direction. 'They're going to talk about us,' he said warningly.

Diane tucked her hand under Jo's elbow, gave her a conspiratorial nod and said to Conrad as they walked away. 'Don't be such an egotist. I can't think of a more boring topic of conversation.'

She chatted about nonconsequential topics with Jo as she led her into the house, past the spacious brown and gold kitchen where the caterers were organising the salads that would be brought out when the steaks were finished, through the wide living room with its huge stone fireplace and expanse of gold carpet, and up the stairs to the rose and slate blue master bedroom where she closed the door and said with a sigh, 'Finally, now we can talk.'

'I . . .'

'I know you're going to think I'm a busybody,' Diane said, 'but I can't help worrying . . . oh, look, why don't you sit down. I'm not being much of a hostess.'

Jo sat obediently down on the stool by the vanity table with its assortment of crystal pots and glass perfume bottles while Diane perched on the edge of the king-size bed, her small frame barely making a dint in the huge flower-covered spread. Her slender face with its wide brown eyes had turned from smiling to intensely serious, and Jo looked at her in confusion.

'I just can't help being concerned,' Diane said. 'We've known Conrad for years; he's been like an uncle to our kids; and he and Frank have been very close in business. I guess I have a sort of maternal feeling towards him, and I'd just like to make sure that he's happy.' She paused and then rushed on, not giving Jo a chance to get a word in edgeways, 'He hasn't been, you know, and I don't mean to interfere, but if your reason for coming has been simply to keep him hanging...' She stopped and gave Jo a shameful look. 'Oh, God, I am being an interfering busybody, and I know it's not a bit of my business, but please accept what I say in a friendly way. Conrad could never be happy living in the East. It would be a terrible mistake for him to leave; he was brought up in the prairies—it's his world. And New York! That would be a real disaster. He'd suffocate there, he'd be miserable and he'd make you wretched. I just know it. So if you're here to persuade him to leave, please think it over.'

The rush of words came to an abrupt halt, and the two women stared at one another, Diane with entreaty in her eyes, Jo looking completely baffled. 'I'm sorry,' she finally said. 'But I'm afraid that I don't have a clue...'

Diane spread her hands in a gesture of pleading. 'I know that I'm not being very articulate, but it's such a difficult subject and I've really no right to get between the two of you. It's just so obvious that you and Conrad wouldn't last a minute together. And it isn't that you're not a nice person; I'm sure you are, but you're not right for Conrad if you can't make a home with him out here.' She shook her blonde curls in frustration. 'I know I sound like an idiot, but am I making any sense?'

Jo shook her head helplessly. 'Not a lot,' she admitted. 'I think you must have the wrong woman.'

There was a brief moment of silence while Diane stared at her and then said, 'Aren't you from New York?'

'Upstate New York, not the City.'

'And didn't you meet Conrad two years ago in Vancouver?'

'No.'

'Oh!' There was a long stretch of silence while Diane's face registered an assortment of facial expressions ranging from astonishment through bewilderment to a red blush of embarrassment. 'You mean you're not Marion,' she said slowly.

'I'm Jo Davidson. Conrad introduced us.'

'I . . . I guess I wasn't listening very closely when he said your name. I was so sure that . . . God, I've really made a mess of things, haven't I?'

'That's . . . all right.' Now that Jo was over her confusion, the gist of Diane's words were starting to hit home.

'It's just that I knew you were from New York and I put two and two together and came up with five.' She paused. 'If you're not Marion, then when did you meet Conrad?'

Jo went for the simplest story. 'At the Pincher Creek Hospital about three weeks ago. My sister broke her ankle camping and met Paul there. The Wyatts are putting us up until she's well enough to drive home.'

'Please forget all I said then. It was so . . . stupid.'

But Jo had no intention of forgetting Diane's words and she said in a casual tone, 'Conrad gets letters from a woman in Manhattan.'

Diane sighed. 'Oh, that's Marion all right. Conrad met her in Vancouver and the next thing we knew they had a hot and heavy pen-pal relationship. I probably gave you the idea that I know what's going on between them, but I really don't. It's all guesswork, based on the fact that Conrad has actually mentioned Marion to Frank and me. He doesn't usually talk about the women he goes out with and we rarely meet any. I wanted to meet Marion, but the one time she came to Calgary, we were on vacation. Then Conrad went to New York and came back looking like a dark thundercloud. I'm afraid my brain went on overtime and I assumed that Marion won't come west and Conrad won't settle in the East.'

Jo made a wry grimace. 'He doesn't have a high opinion of Easterners.'

'They're a different breed.' Diane noticed Jo's look of disbelief. 'They really are, you know. I've got culture shock just visiting Toronto. I can't get used to skyscrapers, endless pavement and people who are too busy to give you the time of day.'

'Not everyone's like that,' Jo protested. 'I come from a small town and it's so friendly it verges on claustrophobic.'

Diane gave a resigned shrug. 'Well, it was obvious to all of us that Conrad's long distance romance wasn't going well, and when he said he was bringing a visitor from New York to the barbecue tonight, I naturally assumed you were the woman in question. And you look like the type Conrad usually goes for, too.' She stood up, adding, 'We'd better get back or the men will send a posse out after us.'

But the intimation that she was part of a crowd of Conrad-worshipers made Jo uneasy and she didn't budge. 'And what type is that?' she asked.

Diane glanced in the mirror over the vanity, rearranged one curl by her ear and patted her hair with a satisfied expression. 'Tall, brunette, pretty. Conrad never had a taste for blondes.' She turned and gave Jo an impish grin. 'Like me.'

The food was being served when they returned to the patio, and the waiters were putting the final touches on tables that dotted the lawn, covering them with pink, blue and yellow tablecloths and giving each a floral centrepiece with a candle in the middle. Jo couldn't find Conrad in the crowd that had formed around the barbecue area so she stood near the back, watching the guests and trying to concentrate on their conversations. The weather, she noticed, seemed to be the dominant topic.

'The trouble with Calgary,' one woman to her left was saying, 'is the climate. I'd move here in a minute if it weren't for the winters.'

A man next to her laughed, 'Then you haven't seen the hail we can get in June.'

'Hail in June?'

'The size of golf balls, bouncing all over the grass on the front lawn and sounding as if they'd break down the roof.'

'I don't believe it,' she said. 'You're pulling my leg.'

But Jo couldn't keep her mind on the oddities of the Calgary climate. Her thoughts kept straying back to Diane's words, and she began to realise how much more logical Conrad's antipathy to anything eastern seemed to be now that she knew about Marion. She could just imagine their relationship with Conrad's down-to-earth philosophy pitted against Marion's Manhattan sophistication. It must have been explosive. She had to agree with Diane; she couldn't, not for even a second, imagine Conrad living in New York City. He was a man that one associated with sun, wind and the pleasures of wide open spaces, not with enclosed offices, pavement and the frantic hustle-bustle of Manhattan. He was not an urban man; she'd seen him coming back from riding around his property, his hair dampened with sweat from riding in the sun, his face raw from the abrasive whip of the wind, his demeanour content and satisfied. He was more at home in jeans than a suit and, although he made his living from business, Jo suspected that his words to her earlier that day had not been spoken in jest. He probably did prefer to be 'riding the range' rather than fighting corporate battles.

Still, it was obvious that Conrad was attracted to women who carried an aura of urban elegance on them with the ease that they wore perfume. How else could he have fallen for a woman who wrote letters on lightly scented mauve stationery, her handwriting delicate and flowing? Conrad, Diane had said, went for women who were tall, dark and pretty, and Jo could just envision

Marion in her mind's eye, dressed in designer fashions, expertly made-up and capable of witty and urbane conversation. Perhaps, she thought, it was the contrast that Conrad liked. Opposites attract after all, and what could be more interesting and enticing to a man brought up on the harsh prairies than a woman whose idea of the great outdoors was a quick dash from one building to the next, from the hairdresser to the couturier, from her apartment to the theatre.

'A steak for your thoughts.'

Jo turned to find Roddy standing beside her, his outstretched hand holding a platter with a sizzling steak on it at least two inches thick. 'Uh-uh,' Jo said, shaking her head. 'I couldn't eat half of that.'

He grinned at her. 'It's the only size they serve— gigantic.'

Jo reluctantly took the plate. 'Is this what they mean by western hospitality?'

'Generous,' he said, nodding and then waving a hand over in the direction of one of the tables. 'Care to join me?'

'I . . . well, I thought I'd be sitting with Conrad . . .'

'He's already found himself a bevy of adoring females.' Roddy gestured towards a crowd on the patio, and Jo saw the gleam of Conrad's gold hair among the assorted brunette, redhead and blonde of five laughing women.

'Oh.'

'So you'll join me?'

Jo looked deliberately away from Conrad and smiled at Roddy. 'Why not?' she said. She didn't care if Conrad hadn't sought her out and preferred the company of other women to her own. She was quite capable of enjoying herself with or without his presence.

'Frankly,' Roddy said as he took Jo by the elbow and led her in the direction of the empty table, 'I'm considering growing a moustache if that's all it takes to attract women.'

Jo tilted her head, ascertained his features and finally said, 'I think you'd look funny with a moustache.'

'Funny? Not distinguished or dashing or sexy?' Roddy looked crestfallen as he pulled out a chair beside her and put his plate on the table.

Jo patted his hand. 'You're fine just the way you are.'

There was a short silence as they started to carve their steaks and then Roddy began to enquire about her family. 'Bring me up to date on the news. You have a sister, don't you?'

'Emily—she's four years younger than I am.'

'And where is she?'

'Here, too.'

'Here in Calgary?'

'We were camping near Pincher Creek and she broke her ankle. She met Paul Wyatt in the hospital and the next thing I knew we were houseguests.'

'Hmmm.' He gave her a shrewd look. 'You don't sound too happy about it.'

'Did you know Emily?'

'Let me think. A little blonde thing. A sweet smile.'

'A little naïve and inexperienced, too.'

'Oh, I get it,' Roddy said. 'She's fallen under the renowned Wyatt charm.'

'She thinks she's in love with Paul.'

'I don't know Paul too well.'

'The point,' Jo said, as she viciously speared a piece of steak, 'is that we have to leave in a few weeks to go back to New York and nothing's going to come of it.'

'What's wrong with a little fun?'

'Now, that's a typical male attitude,' she said coldly.

'Don't get your back up, Jo. A little romance is good for the soul. It clears the brain, gets rid of the fuzzy edges and the cobwebs. It'll put Emily on her toes for a while, and she'll have a great time.'

'And what about afterwards?'

He shrugged. 'Since she knows it's temporary . . .'

'Roddy, you don't know the first thing about women. You haven't changed in the least.'

He put his fork down and looked at her indignantly. 'Now, what does that mean?'

Jo wiggled a finger under his nose. 'I remember that crush you had on Megan Scofield in high school. You gave her rocks instead of flowers for the prom.'

'They were good geological specimens,' he asserted. '*I* certainly would have preferred them to flowers.'

Jo couldn't help laughing. 'Honestly, Roddy, you were such a sap.'

He gave her a broad grin. 'I was, wasn't I?'

'Really.'

'Jo, are you hooked up with Conrad in any way?'

She shook her head. 'No, I'm just a houseguest.'

'There's no reason why you can't get out and have a little fun, is there?'

'Well, I . . .'

'How about an honest-to-goodness date? Come with me to see the rodeo at the Stampede on Sunday night?'

Jo was about to say no when she suddenly thought of the small pile of mauve envelopes that had graced the small table in the foyer during Conrad's absence, mute testimony to an affair that had been, according to Diane, going on for two years and for all Jo knew was still in full force. 'Sure,' she said slowly, and then gave Roddy a dazzling smile. 'I'd love to.'

CHAPTER FIVE

CONRAD found his way to Jo and Roddy's table during dessert, apologised for getting caught up with some acquaintances during dinner and spent the next half-hour discussing Roddy's recent attempt to get the environmentalists and mining executives together. Although they were philosophically on opposite sides of the fence, neither he nor Roddy seemed to hold any antagonism against one another, despite the fact that their conversation was sprinkled with disagreement and the occasional nasty jibe. Politics, Jo realised, makes odd bedfellows and none seemed odder than Conrad with his very western philosophy of 'may the best man win' and Roddy with his eastern liberalism that espoused government regulation and involvement.

As the sun lowered itself over the peak of the horizon, Jo and Conrad made their goodbyes to the Beauchamps and headed back to the Wyatt ranch. They talked for a while about the barbecue and then Conrad surprised Jo by also asking her to the opening rodeo of the Stampede.

'I'm sorry,' she said, 'but Roddy's already asked me to go.'

Conrad gave her a sideways glance as he negotiated the car around a tight curve. 'You seem like great friends.'

'That's what happens when two people from the same small town meet somewhere else. It's like a homecoming.'

'You mean you weren't great friends before?'

'Acquaintances is the best word, I guess. We've known one another for years.'

'The way you did Douglas?'

Jo swivelled in her chair and looked at Conrad in astonishment. 'Douglas?' she echoed.

'Your ex.'

'*Who* told you about Douglas?'

'Your small town seems to have been a hotbed of sex and intrigue.'

Jo sat back against her seat, her mouth pressed together in a tight line. 'I'm going to kill Emily.'

A small amused smile tugged at Conrad's lips. 'You can't do that.'

'Oh, can't I?'

'You're here to protect her, remember?'

Conrad's mockery went right over Jo's head as she considered Emily's perfidy. How could *she*? How dared she tell the Wyatts about Douglas? How could Emily have brought herself to reveal to *strangers* the intimate and unhappy details of Jo's life? Jo cringed inwardly when she considered that Conrad now had, at his fingertips, enough ammunition to humiliate her for the rest of her life. She clenched her hands on the soft leather of her purse, her fingernails digging into a seam, her eyes staring straight ahead of her, her back straight and rigid. She never changed position, not even when Conrad drove the car up the long, curving drive before the Wyatt house and then around to the back where the garages were situated.

'Jo?' he said after he had clicked off the engine and she still sat in silent rigidity. 'Look, Jo—it doesn't matter.'

She didn't look at him. 'What doesn't matter?'

'What this guy did to you.'

Her voice was small. 'It matters to me.'

'You were young then and innocent . . .'

'Stupid and gullible,' she completed, her voice bitter. 'I know all the grounds I can plead, Conrad, but it doesn't change what happened.'

'The point is—you can't judge every man by Douglas' behaviour.'

'That's easy enough to say. Have *you* ever been

burned in a love affair?' She turned to look at him then, confronting him full face and saw that his grey eyes were serious, looking at her levelly beneath the golden eyebrows.

'Yes,' he said, 'I have.'

For a moment Jo was almost willing to be pulled into an atmosphere of mutual sympathy and understanding. She would have liked to know what kind of a woman was capable of breaking Conrad's heart, what sort of power she must have wielded to bring a man of Conrad's confidence and masculinity to his knees, but Jo resisted the desire to ask. She didn't want to make a reciprocal confession. She didn't want to have to explain about Douglas, and she didn't need Conrad's comfort.

'Then you can understand, I'm sure, why I don't want to talk about it and why I wish Emily had kept her mouth shut.'

Conrad stretched one arm across the back of the car seat so that his fingers almost touched Jo's shoulder. 'It's interesting how both you and Emily work so hard at taking care of one another.'

Jo pulled back against the car door. 'I don't think "taking care of me" includes talking about my love life.'

'But she did it in defence, you know. She was merely trying to make me understand what makes you tick.'

'I'm going to have a small talk with Emily and let her know ...'

Conrad touched her shoulder then, his fingers warm against the thin fabric of her blouse. 'You and Emily are closer than most sisters. You live together, don't you?'

'It's cheaper to live that way.'

'And you take your vacations together.'

'I happen to enjoy Emily's company more than anyone else's.'

'You seem to live in one another's pockets.'

Jo straightened up, inadvertently forcing her shoulder into the palm of his hand. 'I really don't see anything wrong with the way I live or the way I treat my sister. She's my flesh-and-blood and I care about her and want the best for her. It's not an emotion to be laughed at or scorned, and I don't understand why you find it odd or peculiar.'

The thumb of the hand resting on her shoulder made small circular motions against the bared curve of her collarbone. 'It's not the caring or concern that bothers me,' Conrad said. 'It's the way you want to isolate both you and Emily from the rest of the world. It isn't healthy.'

Jo tried to ignore the sensations that arose from the feel of his hand on her skin. 'I want to isolate Emily from men who may hurt her.'

The last of the sun sent a shaft of warm orange light through the front windshield of the car and lit Conrad's hair into a fiery gold. 'May I assume that you're referring to Paul?'

'You may assume that,' she replied coldly.

'Why do you think he'll hurt her?'

'Do I have to spell it out for you? Isn't it obvious?'

'No, it isn't.'

'Paul met Emily in the hospital when she was hurt, tired and alone. I wouldn't have minded a little flirtation—after all, she needed the diversion, but Paul didn't stop there. He invited her to stay in the house, he's showering her with attention and he's leading her down a rosy path of illusions. At some point soon, Emily's going to have to come down to reality and it's going to hurt.'

'What makes you think that Paul isn't just as infatuated as Emily?'

'He may be,' she conceded, 'but his future is here and hers isn't. Paul isn't risking anything. Don't you see?'

His hand had moved to the curve of her neck above her collarbone where a slender chain of gold lay against her skin. He picked it up with his thumb and forefinger and idly rubbed it between them. 'It's clear to me that Paul has fallen head-over-heels in love with your sister.

In fact, it worries me. Paul has a lot of schooling to get through before he can start work, and I don't like the idea of him getting emotionally involved to the point that he won't finish what he's started.'

Although Jo should have been relieved that Conrad was just as opposed to a serious relationship between Emily and Paul as she was, his words had the opposite effect. 'If you don't think my sister is good enough for your . . .'

'Hold it, New York.' He let her gold chain fall back against her neck and his fingers pulled away, but not before his knuckles grazed the top of her breasts, and she shivered in spite of herself at that touch. 'Emily's a nice girl but . . .'

Jo fiinished his words for him. 'I know,' she said bitterly, 'she can't measure up to the Wyatt standard of wealth and station.'

For a moment Conrad gazed at her in silence and then he said, 'Is that another chip you've been carrying around on your shoulder?'

Jo was willing to admit that her attitude was based partially on jealousy, but she also knew that Conrad had no real idea of what her life was like. It had always struck her as ironic that while the poor could easily imagine how the wealthy lived, the reverse wasn't true at all. The rich could never imagine what it was like to worry about meeting car payments or not having enough extra cash to buy a much-needed dress or being budgeted so tightly that when hamburgers went up ten cents a pound a vegetarian diet was the only answer.

Still, she wanted to make Conrad understand so she said, 'My family is poor, and neither Emily nor I have received financial help from either of our parents. We both got through school on student loans, and we're still paying them off. I don't know what they pay starting kindergarten teachers in Alberta, but I can assure you that what Emily makes barely pays for the rent on our apartment. My salary is somewhat more generous, but basically we're scraping by. If I'd had the money, I would have flown Emily home, not thrown the both of us on your hospitality.' Jo couldn't help it; she spat the last word out as if it were a piece of dirt.

'That's really bugging you, isn't it?' he said quietly, his eyes resting on her flushed face.

'I've met people like you, Conrad,' Jo went on, her voice passionate. 'It isn't that you think money grows on trees, but you make assumptions about security that comes from a confidence based on having more than enough to get by. Look at your friends the Beauchamps with their big house and steaks enough to feed the entire Asian continent. Money will cushion them from any fall, but it won't cushion Emily and me. When we go back to New York and she discovers that her summer romance with Paul was merely a dalliance on his part, she isn't going to be able to get away from it all or have a nice restful breakdown. She's going to have to face twenty-five four year olds for eight hours a day.'

'Damned if you don't have more prickles than a porcupine.'

Jo felt his inward smile and it made her even more angry, more vehement. She put her hand on the door handle, but she wanted to get her point across before she got out. 'Just understand,' she said, her chin high and her amber eyes flashing, 'that I don't plan to owe you a thing. We'll be getting out of here just as soon as we can and I'll send you a cheque for room and board when I get the money together. Emily and I may not have much but we don't believe in reneging on our debts. You've been very kind, but we are, after all, strangers, and I don't expect anything from strangers except . . .'

'God, New York,' he drawled, 'but you sure do go on.'

His arms were around her and his mouth was on hers before Jo even had a chance to move. She was still filled with her indignant wrath and the belief that she must tell Conrad in full all the things she had stored in outrage and unhappiness during the past two weeks, so she fought his embrace and the feel of his lips on hers, fought the sudden comfort of strong arms and a broad chest, fought all the tender warmth of his hands caressing her back. She struggled and wiggled so much that Conrad finally loosened his arms and, leaning back, looked into her eyes.

'I had an idea,' he said with a hint of laughter in his voice, 'that kissing you wasn't going to be easy.'

Jo had put her hands up against his chest to keep him away. 'I don't think it's funny,' she said indignantly.

'You need to develop a better sense of humour. Life isn't so serious.'

'That's easy enough for you to say.'

'All right, let's put it another way. Life is damned serious, but if you can't laugh at it once in a while then it's going to look pretty bleak.'

Jo gave him the full benefit of her angriest glare. 'I don't want to get involved with you—it would be pointless. In less than two weeks, we'll go our separate ways and no affair . . .'

'New York, I was only going to kiss you!'

Jo flushed and Conrad took advantage of her hesitation to pull her into his arms again. This time she felt all the sensations that he'd intended her to feel. The hard line of his mouth was softer than she would have thought; his dark-gold moustache was rough and masculine against her skin. His head bent over hers blocked the lowering sun and Jo closed her eyes, her hands resting lightly against his chest, her fingertips sensing the steady beat of his heart through the fabric of his shirt. It was only a short kiss, a brief and tantalising meeting of their lips, and he cut it surprisingly short, pulling back and saying as he did so, 'There, that didn't hurt, did it?'

He sounded so much like a parent chiding a toddler that even Jo had to smile. 'It was painless, Mr Wyatt,' she conceded.

'Then the next one . . .'

'Oh, no,' she said quickly. 'That was quite sufficient.'

'I have a way of breaking in wild horses,' he said with a grin. 'Have I told you about it?'

The abrupt change of subject startled Jo. 'No, I . . .'

'I like the slow and easy method; it makes them more docile.'

Jo suddenly got the odious metaphor and pushed Conrad abruptly and with all the force she could muster against the chest so that he was forced to sit back beside the wheel. He was laughing as she opened the car door, got out and slammed it hard behind her, and she would have marched off indignantly if it weren't for the sound of his laughter. Instead she stuck her head in through the open window and said through clenched teeth, 'I've never been docile in my life and I don't plan to start now—no matter what sort of strategy you try.'

Conrad put his hands up in the air as if surrendering. 'Okay, New York, you win.'

'And keep this in mind,' she went on, bound and determined to have the last word, 'I'm a lot smarter than a horse, too.'

Jo fumed all the way into the house, up the stairs and into her bedroom where she sat down on the bed and stared at the wall in frustration and irritation. One minute Conrad was easy to get along with; the next he was difficult and finally he ended up laughing at her. It seemed to make no difference to Jo how she acted, he always seemed to get the better of her. Comparing her to a *horse*—he really had a lot of nerve. She pulled her hair out of its chignon, ran her fingers through the falling strands of hair and pushed them away from her face. Conrad's behaviour during the evening had puzzled her; he had asked her to the barbecue and then left her on her own. He hadn't seemed the least put out when he learned that Roddy had already invited her out for the rodeo. And then, when it should have been clear to both of them that their relationship was merely that of acquaintances, he'd made his first pass. It really didn't make much sense.

Unless, of course, he was doing precisely what he had said—treating her the way he'd treat some stubborn bronco, playing her loose and easy, giving her plenty of lead and only tightening the rope gently when she relaxed. The idea of it made Jo even angrier and she stood up and walked over to her closet, throwing open the door and staring at her meagre belongings before she unbuttoned her blouse. As she had expected, her small lecture to Conrad on the state of her and Emily's resources had gone right over his handsome, blond head. Jo didn't really know why she had bothered to explain. He really had no idea of the way she worried about finances and the difficulties they had making ends meet. He couldn't begin to understand what it had been like to spend a childhood wearing cousins' hand-me-downs and making do with bicycles and dolls from rummage sales. Conrad had been brought up in the lap of luxury while Jo and Emily had spent a good portion of their childhood only semi-protected by the kindness of a social worker and the monthly welfare cheque. The rest of the time they were subject to the fortunes of Prudence whose ability to manage money and keep a job had always been precarious.

It was all right for Conrad to insist that she have sense of humour, but Jo had unfortunately had it knocked out of her at an early stage of her life. Her father had left the family not quite starving but almost penniless, and his cheques, which had first come at regular intervals, had finally tapered off as the years went by. It wasn't that he was particularly cruel or mean, but Jo suspected that he'd finally married someone else and had another family to support. He'd left Prudence when Jo was only five and Emily one, and she supposed that the normal emotional connections between a father and his daughters had never developed strongly enough for him to feel responsible for them. She'd understood Paul's bitterness about his mother—she had felt the same way about her father for years. Emily, of course, had not, but then she couldn't remember the tall man who, when he came home from work, would throw them into the air, one after the other, laughing when they would begin to shriek both from the joy of flying next to the ceiling and the fear that they would fall without the safety of his arms.

Prudence had, quite literally, come apart after he had gone, and Jo and Emily had been taken care of by sympathetic neighbours until the social agency took them in hand. It was during that time that Jo had become so attached to her baby sister, unwilling to be parted from her and so fiercely protective that the social worker had decided that it was far more important to keep the family together than to send the sisters to separate foster homes. Prudence had finally dragged herself out of her depression, taken night courses to train for secretarial work and been hired by the telephone company. That job had only lasted for a few months until she had another depressive episode, but little by little her jobs lasted longer and the interval of time between one breakdown and the next lengthened until she was finally supporting the girls on her own. By that time Jo was in high school and had a part-time job delivering papers during the winter and a summer job working in the records department of a nearby hospital.

It was, Jo thought to herself, as she stepped out of her skirt and pulled her nightgown over her head, a harder existence than most children experienced and its repercussions were many. She'd lost her sense of humour; she'd developed a chip on her shoulder of immense proportions and she'd been taught early in life that no one was trustworthy—certainly not a father that could walk away from his children and never return, or a mother who was so weak that she collapsed at the first sign of adversity. They were tough lessons for a young girl to learn, but Jo had been an avid student. If she was tough and hard now, she had good reason, and nothing Conrad did or said was going to prove to her that she should trust him anymore than she had trusted, at what must have been the weakest moment of her life, Douglas Bannock.

Thinking about Douglas brought Jo up short, and sent her mind in the direction of Emily. It was about time, she decided as she grabbed a bathrobe that Mrs Beattie had provided for her and walked towards the bedroom door, that she had a talk with Emily: a heart-to-heart, down-to-earth talk. They hadn't talked in a long time, not since that last conversation in the hospital when Emily had insisted that she would stay with the Wyatts rather than go home to Prudence. Jo had thought it made good sense to keep away from Emily, to let her know that she was on her own, to give her the feeling that she was responsible for her own life. It hadn't occurred to Jo that giving Emily the space to be her own person meant that she would suddenly turn into a blabbermouth about Jo's personal experiences, but if that's what was happening, then she'd damned well make sure that Emily wouldn't talk again.

She found Emily with Paul in her bedroom. They were watching television, both fully dressed and lying on top of the bedspread, propped up against some pillows. Paul had his arm around Emily's shoulders, and Emily was leaning against him, looking content and comfortable in his embrace, her soft blonde hair tumbling on to his plaid shirt. They both looked up when Jo stalked in, and something in her face must have shown them the lay of the land, because Paul got up in a hurry, said a quick good night to both of them and was out of the door in a few minutes. Emily sat there looking apprehensive as Jo clicked off the television and then turned to her.

'Is anything the matter, Jo?'

'What do you think?'

'I thought you were going to the barbecue. Didn't you have a good time?'

Jo sat down on a chair by Emily's bed. 'The barbecue was fine.'

'And Conrad?'

'Fine, too.' She paused. 'I met Roddy Moore there.'

'Roddy? You mean Roddy from Fairfax?'

Jo nodded. 'He's taking me to the rodeo on Sunday night.'

Emily gave her a wary glance. 'That's nice, isn't it?'

'Do you think so?'

Emily clasped her small hands together. 'Jo, you're mad at me, aren't you?'

Jo leaned back in the chair. 'Furious,' she admitted.

'Is it something I did? Something I said?'

'Something you said.'

'To who? To Paul? To Conrad?'

'To Conrad.'

'What could I have said to Conrad that . . .' Her voice trailed off and her mouth formed a small O.

'Right,' Jo said grimly.

'He asked me about you; he wanted to know what made you so unhappy.' Emily gave Jo a quick glance and then looked away. 'You are unhappy, you know.'

'And you had to tell him about Douglas.'

'I only said that you'd had a bad love affair, that Douglas had left you—that's all that I said. I didn't go into details.'

Jo stared into her sister's face and saw the helpful innocence written across it. Her anger towards Emily was deflating rapidly; she had always found it difficult to be angry with her sister—she was too accustomed to caring for her and protecting her—but she wished fervently that Emily had not spoken to Conrad. 'Em, how could you?'

'It's not a state secret, and it's not so terrible. Lots of people have affairs that go bad, Jo. You're not the only one.'

'But Conrad,' Jo said helplessly, 'of all people.'

Emily examined her nails. 'Do you like him?'

'Who—Conrad? He's . . . he's all right.'

'I think he's sexy, don't you?'

'Listen, Em, if you and Paul are busy matchmaking, you can forget it. I'm not interested.'

'I think Conrad is interested.'

Jo shook her head impatiently. 'Conrad already has a girl-friend.'

'Who?'

'A woman who lives in Manhattan.'

Emily waved her hand in the air as if to flick Marion off into outer space. 'Oh, her. Paul told me about her. That's over and done with.'

'He's still getting mail from her.'

'Paul says she's persistent.'

Jo looked at Emily in some exasperation. She supposed that neither Emily nor Paul could resist trying to connive a romance between Conrad and herself, but she was going to put an end to it tonight. There was no telling how far they would go if she didn't. 'I have no intentions of getting involved with Conrad—period.'

Emily's blue eyes were shrewd. 'You don't think he's the tiniest bit sexy?'

'He's very attractive,' Jo said firmly, 'but that doesn't make any difference. I plan to go back to New York with my heart free.'

Emily's mouth tightened. 'Are you referring to me?'

'Well, Em, is your heart free?'

'Not in the slightest,' she said defiantly, 'and it makes me very happy.'

Although Jo had promised herself that she wouldn't interfere in Emily's doings, she couldn't resist the chance to advise her sister once again. 'You're going to be miserable when we leave,' she said gently. 'Transcontinental romances have a habit of dying off. It's hard to stay in love and be true when your only contact is the mailman.'

'I would say that it depends on the quality of the love.'

'Every person in love thinks no one else can have experienced the same thing. The irony is that it's universal.'

'I hate it when you laugh at me. I'm not thirteen, you know.'

'I'm not laughing at you. I'm just feeling sorry for you in advance, Em. I know just what you're going to go through.'

Emily flung her hair back over her shoulders. 'You are not the expert, Jo. In fact, I'd say you're a novice at the whole business. One lousy boy-friend doesn't entitle you to be patronising.'

Jo saw that she was being too heavy-handed and she tried hastily to make amends. 'I'm sorry if I sound patronising. I don't mean to; I just want to be helpful. We'll be leaving here in less than two weeks and . . .'

'Maybe I won't go.'

Jo's breath seemed to have been knocked out of her and she stared at Emily, taking in the flush on her chesks, the demure cut of her white blouse with its round Peter Pan collar and her jeans with one leg cut off to accommodate the white bulk of her cast. Paul had written on the cast, drawing a large amateurish heart over the knee with an arrow sticking through it and a scrawled 'I Love You' written inside with purple ink. 'What do you mean?' she asked slowly. 'What do you mean you won't go?'

Emily wasn't looking at her; she was staring down at her bare toes. 'Maybe I'll stay in Calgary.'

'But . . . you don't have a job here.'

'I could find one.'

'You're not a Canadian citizen.'

'I could get papers.'

'How? It's not so easy now. The Canadian government doesn't hand out immigration papers to anyone who wants them.'

'I could get them easily . . . if I married Paul.'

She didn't know why she was so shocked or why a hand seemed to tighten around her heart in a painful fist. She should have seen it coming; it had been written across Emily's face for days. 'You're crazy,' she whispered.

Emily shook her head vehemently, her eyes bright. 'I've wanted to tell you for ages, but Paul said I shouldn't. But don't you see, Jo, how perfect it will be? Paul can go to school, and I can go to work. Calgary is an expanding city and there are lots of job opportunities. I won't even have to worry about my medical expenses once I'm a landed immigrant. The province covers the doctors' fees.' She paused and Jo, seeing that her excitement and enthusiasm were bubbling over, wondered how many hours Paul and Emily had spent together, planning their future through the most roseate of glasses.

'You've known Paul for three weeks,' she said.

Emily leaned forward. 'Jo, it was love at first sight. It really was.'

'You're both young. How do you know . . .'

'I love him.' The words were said with sincerity and dignity, and Jo knew that arguing against Emily's emotions would be fighting a losing battle so she desperately tried another tack.

'Paul has years of business school before he finishes his degree. He shouldn't saddle himself with a wife.'

'Lots of undergraduate students have wives.'

Another desperate tack. 'A little bit of separation wouldn't hurt, Em. It would be one way of proving . . .'

'Paul and I know what we want.'

Jo felt as if she kept coming up against a brick wall and hitting her head against its hard and implacable surface. She saw that nothing she could say was going to change Emily's mind, and a sense of panic pervaded her. She couldn't imagine living without her sister. They'd been together for so long, had got along together so well . . .

'Would you do me a favour, Em?' Jo pleaded. 'Would you please not make a decision for a few more weeks? You have plenty of time and I won't object if I know that you and Paul have thought it through some more.'

Emily shrugged. 'It isn't going to make any difference, you know.'

Jo put out her hands beseechingly. 'I don't know

that. Perhaps you and Paul will quarrel and discover that you're not perfect for one another. Really, Em, think about it. You hardly know one another.'

Emily lifted her chin. 'We know each other very well.'

'Three weeks is hardly long enough for . . .' Jo's voice trailed off when the implications of Emily's words hit home, and she stared at her sister with a look of stunned disbelief on her face.

'I'm sorry, but it's true.' There was a touch of something in Emily's voice that reminded Jo of her sister long ago when she had got into a childish scrape and, rather than accept punishment, would defiantly insist that she couldn't help what she had done.

'You haven't.'

'Yes, we have.'

'For how long?'

Emily gave her a small, secretive smile. 'Well, we didn't in the hospital.'

Jo rolled her eyes towards the ceiling. 'It's nice to know you had some common sense,' she said sarcastically.

'It was a few days after we came here. One afternoon when you'd gone for a long walk.'

Jo remembered all those long, lonely walks she had taken because she hadn't wanted to act the role of overbearing chaperon. While she had spent hours walking through fields of long, prairie grass and pondering on the difficulties of the future, Emily had allowed Paul to make love to her, throwing her allegiance to Jo into the winds and risking . . .

'Emily, you could be pregnant!'

'Uh-uh. Paul knew exactly what to do.' She paused, looking into Jo's despairing face and then said, 'He's really wonderful, you know. Paul wouldn't hurt me for the world, and I'm glad, really glad, that we've gone to bed together because now I know for sure that we're right for one another.' Her voice softened. 'Jo, it wasn't awkward or terrible or frightening. It was truly one of the most beautiful things . . .'

Jo couldn't bear it for one more minute. She stood up abruptly, pushing the chair back with a rough sound. 'I'll see you tomorrow, Em,' she said, hoping that none of her emotions showed on her face or could be heard in the imminent cracking of her voice.

'Jo! Are you okay?'

'Fine,' she said as she made it to the bedroom door. 'Sleep tight.'

It was one of their family expressions and it made tears suddenly come to Emily's eyes. 'Jo, please don't leave. You have to understand . . .'

But Jo had closed the door on that soft, pleading voice. She could no longer listen to the things Emily wished to remember or watch her sister's face soften in reminiscence. She barely made it to her room before she felt the cry build in her throat with a painful, unswallowable pressure, and she threw herself on to the bed, pushing her face into a pillow so that no one would be able to hear the harsh sounds of her weeping.

Jo hardly ever cried. Prudence's breakdowns had found her dry-eyed; Douglas' betrayal had cost her great anguish but not one single tear. In fact, in the Davidson family, Jo was known to be capable of enduring even the worst cuts and bruises, the most serious set-backs and problems, without an emotion crossing her face. But on this night Jo cried her heart out. She cried for all the memories she had of Emily as a baby with pudgy fat arms and toes and fingers so tiny that Jo had marvelled over them. She cried for the years that she had got Emily ready in the mornings, twisting her blonde hair into skinny little braids and holding her hand as they had crossed the wide street that ran in front of the elementary school. She cried for the time when Emily had finally grown into adolescence and the night, they had spent together, crawling next to one another under the quilt and talking into the small hours of the morning about teachers and boys and life.

And Jo cried for herself. Not for the loss of Emily's innocence and childhood or the memories that they had shared together. She cried because of the soft glow in Emily's eyes and the wonder in her voice as she had spoken of Paul's lovemaking. In all the time that she had gone out with Douglas Bannock and during the moments she had shared his bed, Jo had never known such wonder or such beauty. She didn't know why that had been so; she had been in love with Douglas or, at least, thought she was, and he had certainly been skilful enough, but beneath it all had been a vast emptiness of feeling and spirit. Emily had been given a gift that she had been denied, and Jo cried for the girl she had been and the sweet illusions she had once held, their loss poignant and painful.

She cried for several hours and then washed her face with cold water and went to bed, turning her pillow over so that its wet side was down. If her eyes were slightly puffy the next morning, no one remarked on their condition, and she acted as if nothing out of the ordinary had occurred, treating Emily and Paul exactly as she had done before and ignoring any of her sister's mute appeals and enquiries. It wasn't in Jo's psychological make-up to search for pity or to let others know that she had been hurt. She was quite accustomed to fending for herself.

CHAPTER SIX

THE Calgary Stampede was everything Jo had ever imagined a western rodeo to be. There was a parade with drum majorettes and girls in white calfskin and fringes twirling batons in the air. There was calf-roping, bucking broncos, clowns and chuckwagon races. There was a sense of fun in the air that was infectious and a letting loose of restraint that made ordinary men turn into macho cowboys wearing white stetsons, chaps and spurs and allowed any woman who had the desire to dress herself up as Calamity Jane. There was a mid-way with roller coasters, ferris wheels and breath-stopping rides for anyone brave enough to risk their lives. The smell of popcorn, hot-dogs and cotton candy was as pervasive as the honky-tonk music that issued from various loudspeakers and the white glare of fluorescent lights that turned every colour into a garish hue and dimmed the stars overhead. Jo and Roddy strolled down a path with booths on each side, and as they passed by a stand where a hawker entreated them 'to some spun candy that would melt in their mouths,' she said, 'If I were about five years old, I would be in seventh heaven.'

'What? You mean you don't want some cotton candy?'

'And risk a dental bill bigger than the national debt?'

As they were sideswiped by a clown with orange hair, a bulbous nose and baggy pants, Roddy said, 'The trouble with you, Jo, is that you never learned how to have fun. I remember you as a solemn little girl and a student who kept her nose to the grindstone.'

Jo shrugged. 'That's the way I am, I guess.'

Roddy stopped, turned around to face Jo, gave her an appraising look and then shook his head. 'Nope,' he said. 'I can see a definite possibility for remodelling.

'Remodelling what?'

'The woman in question. Come with me.' And he took her firmly under the arm and dragged her back to the cotton candy vendor. 'One large,' he announced firmly over Jo's protests and watched with a grin as the man swept the paper cone round and round the large metal container where turquoise sugar was being spun into fine, sticky strands.

'There you are,' he said, presenting her with the enormous blue cloud. 'Give your sweet tooth a break.'

From there, Roddy dragged her over to a shooting gallery where he laid low three ducks and won a large, pink teddy bear with a bright green bow-tie. A ring toss produced a red stetson for her and a ball-throwing game netted her a Stampede flag. Jo put her foot down and refused and be dragged on to rides that were designed to turn her stomach inside-out and upside-down, but by the time they were ready to leave, Roddy's unerring aim and sense of the ridiculous had Jo weighted down with every sort of souvenir and gimmick to be found. She wore a Stampede button on her shirt, a flaming red bandana with a bucking bronco around her neck and an Indian belt whose beaded fringes brushed against the thighs of her jeans as she walked. Her red stetson supported an assortment of buttons and feathers and her arms were full of play animals. She was stuffed to the gills with junk food and by the time they reached Roddy's car, she was groaning.

'I've overdosed,' she said, leaning against the hood as he opened the car. 'I think I'm going to have withdrawal symptoms tomorrow.'

'I thought you liked popcorn.'

'*And* the pizza, the taco chips, the caramel apple, the cotton candy, *ad nauseam* . . . why in God's name did I ever let you talk me into all that stuff.'

'Because I'm such a nice, persuasive fellow. Here let me take some of that stuff.'

Jo willingly dropped the pile of stuffed animals into his

Say Hello to Yesterday
Holly Weston had done it all alone.

She had raised her small son and worked her way up to features writer for a major newspaper. Still the bitterness of the the past seven years lingered.

She had been very young when she married Nick Falconer—but old enough to lose her heart completely when he left. Despite her success in her new life, her old one haunted her.

But it was over and done with—until an assignment in Greece brought her face to face with Nick, and all she was trying to forget. . . .

Time of the Temptress
The game must be played his way!

Rebellion against a cushioned, controlled life had landed Eve Tarrant in Africa. Now only the tough mercenary Wade O'Mara stood between her and possible death in the wild, revolution-torn jungle.

But the real danger was Wade himself—he had made Eve aware of herself as a woman.

"I saved your neck, so you feel you owe me something," Wade said. "But you don't owe me a thing, Eve. Get away from me." She knew she could make him lose his head if she tried. But that wouldn't solve anything. . . .

Your Romantic Adventure Starts Here.

Born Out of Love
It had to be coincidence!

Charlotte stared at the man through a mist of confusion. It was Logan. An older Logan, of course, but unmistakably the man who had ravaged her emotions and then abandoned her all those years ago.

She ought to feel angry. She ought to feel resentful and cheated. Instead, she was apprehensive—terrified at the complications he could create.

"We are not through, Charlotte," he told her flatly. "I sometimes think we haven't even begun."

Man's World
Kate was finished with love for good.

Kate's new boss, features editor Eliot Holman, might have devastating charms—but Kate couldn't care less, even if it was obvious that he was interested in her.

Everyone, including Eliot, thought Kate was grieving over the loss of her husband, Toby. She kept it a carefully guarded secret just how cruelly Toby had treated her and how terrified she was of trusting men again.

But Eliot refused to leave her alone, which only served to infuriate her. He was no different from any other man. . . or was he?

These FOUR free Harlequin Presents novels allow you to enter the world of romance, love and desire. As a member of the Harlequin Home Subscription Plan, you can continue to experience all the moods of love. You'll be inspired by moments so real...so moving...you won't want them to end. So start your own Harlequin Presents adventure by returning the reply card below. DO IT TODAY!

EXTRA BONUS
MAIL YOUR ORDER
TODAY AND GET A
FREE TOTE BAG
FROM HARLEQUIN.

arms. 'Is there a local orphanage we can donate this to?'

'What? You're not going to place them at the end of your bed and dream about me?'

'I know we acted like a couple of hysterical teenagers, Roddy, but there's a limit to how far I'll go.'

'Gee, and I thought maybe I had,' and he rubbed a booted toe into the ground with mock-adolescent sheepishness, 'a chance.'

They both laughed then and got into the car. Jo sighed with contentment as she leaned her head against the back rest. 'You know, Roddy, I can't remember when I've had more fun.'

Roddy dug the keys out of his jeans and put them in the ignition. 'Would it upset you if I told you I had an underhanded and devious motive for seducing you with popcorn and cotton candy?'

Jo glanced at him. 'No,' she said. 'What motive?'

'I'd like you to make a move on Wyatt.'

'A move?'

Roddy turned to her, his plump face turned serious. 'Of all the coal barons, Wyatt's the most likely to get involved in reclamation. He's open-minded, fair and willing to listen, but I just haven't been able to see him and give him the pitch. It struck me at the Beauchamps, when I realised you were into the environmentalist camp, that you'd be the ideal person to persuade Wyatt to begin a project. I can't get into his office because he's so busy, and you've got him at the dinner table every night.'

'Shame on you, Roddy,' Jo said with a grin. 'And here I thought you'd invited me out for the pleasure of my personality.'

'Hey, I did enjoy being with you!'

'I'm only kidding,' she said, 'but I should have known there was more to the evening than stuffed animals. You always were a political being. I'll never forget those elections in college for sophomore class president. Was there any gimmick you didn't try to get elected?'

Roddy gave her a small smile. 'Not much,' he admitted.

'So you want me to infiltrate the enemy.'

He started up the car. 'Something like that.'

'What makes you think Conrad is even half-way willing to start a reclamation project?'

'Economics—when he took over the mine from his father, the place was running at a loss, coal was at its lowest price in years and no one could blame him for not wanting to throw good money after bad. But rising fuel prices have made coal seem a lot more desirable and the extra money could be used to clean up some of the mess from the 50's and 60's. Wyatt hasn't spent a lot of time on the mine; he's been branching out into more lucrative fields like oil and gas exploration and high-tech, but with the price of coal rising, I think he'll be ripe for some new ideas.'

Jo gave him a curious look as he pulled out of the parking lot. 'I thought your job was apolitical,' she said. 'Strictly a government liaison between all the mining interests.'

'Keep it under your hat, but I'm going to be leaving the government soon. It looks like the conservation people have got enough money together to hire me as a consultant.'

'Very nice,' she said.

He shrugged. 'It's more money and it's time I settled down.'

'Settled down?'

'I never thought I'd stay in Alberta,' he said, 'but the days turned into months, the months into years and I'm still here. I'm part of the network now and, well, I like the life out here. You don't have to be a cowboy to appreciate the place. I've applied for Canadian citizenship and,' he paused and gave Jo another sheepish look, 'I've sprung the question to a woman I've been dating for about a year.'

'Roddy! You're going to get married!'

'Hard to believe, isn't it?'

'Will wonders never cease?'

'Hey, I didn't have that much of a reputation.'

'Sure you did. It was the opinion of the entire senior class that you were trying to win the medal for "Most Girls Ever Dated".'

'A man's got to give up sometime.'

'And who, may I ask, is the lucky lady?'

Jo couldn't have chosen a more enthusiastic topic for Roddy to discuss. From the time they drove from southwest Calgary to the Wyatt ranch, Roddy talked about the woman in his life. She was a fellow-geologist who worked for the Alberta Department of Energy and Resources, she was tall, blonde and 'not beautiful but attractive', and she was a feminist.

'A feminist?'

Roddy nodded with pride. 'She's a sharp cookie who knows her own mind. In fact, she won't marry me without a contract. We've even got a clause regarding household stuff like taking out the garbage and doing the dishes.'

Jo was silent for a second as she digested Roddy's words. She'd read about such contracts, but she'd never known anyone who'd actually had one. It struck her as odd that Roddy, who came from the most conventional of families, his father was a lawyer, his mother a housewife who kept busy with community affairs, should be willing to start his own on the most unconventional of terms.

'If you don't mind my saying so,' she said, 'I would never have thought you were the kind of man who would go for that sort of thing.'

He threw her a quick glance. 'Why not?'

'You didn't grow up in a family where there was that sort of equality.'

'Maybe it looked that way on the outside,' Roddy said, 'because my mother didn't have a salaried career, but my dad really respected the volunteer work she did, and he was the sort of guy who'd come home at night and pitch in with dinner if she'd been busy all day.'

It gave Jo an odd pang to hear Roddy talk about his parents with such appreciation and affection. There had been nothing like that, of course, in her own family; Prudence hadn't commanded much respect and her father, Jo was sure, had never been the type to help at all. She saw with a sudden clarity that, not only had her childhood made her bitter about marriage, but it had also given her no real understanding of what made a good one work. She could no more imagine what it had been like to live in Roddy's family than she could imagine living on the moon. Like a child at the proverbial candy store window, she would forever be pressing her nose against the glass, the warmth and sweetness out of reach and far out of touch.

The thought made her wince and change the subject. 'Well, a contract hardly sounds—romantic.'

'Oh, we've done the usual moonlight and candlelit dinner route,' he said easily, 'but Maria says there's more to marriage than romance and living happily ever after. It makes sense to me anyway. She's got a tough job and so have I. Why should she be responsible for all the domestic arrangements?'

Jo stole a look at his profile with its slightly bumpy nose and rounded cheek. 'I've never thought of you as "liberated",' she said.

He shrugged as he turned into the Wyatt driveway. 'I don't care much about labels, but I know that I've never liked the type of woman who seems helpless and dependent. Maria's a strong lady and,' he gave Jo a grin, 'I think it's sexy.'

'I guess I can only offer you congratulations and best wishes,' Jo said as he stopped the car in front of the door, 'but it doesn't sound like you need them.'

'You'll work on Wyatt for me?' he said turning to her. 'You don't mind that I wined you and dined you in the hopes of getting you on my side?'

'I'll try. You know where my heart is.'

'Smack dab in every environmentalist squabble. You

always were a fighter, Jo. Rember those debates in college?'

'Very fondly,' she said, leaning over and kissing his cheek. 'Thanks for the evening and I'd like to meet your Maria some day.'

He gave her a hug. 'Don't forget your teddy bear, and keep in touch. I've got a pile of statistics to back up any argument you want to use.'

Jo leaned over to the back seat, swooped up her collection of prizes and eased her way out of the car, pulling her red stetson on to her head. 'I've got lots of my own ammunition,' she said.

'That's what I figured,' Roddy said, and then waving at her, drove away.

Jo juggled the stuffed animals into one arm and let herself into the house, her mind caught up in Roddy's words about his fiancée, Maria. She didn't think that she'd ever met a man who would find an independent woman sexy. Douglas, for example, had preferred that Jo subdue her intellectual acuity and act in what he considered a more feminine manner. And, being infatuated with his position, his wealth and his sophistication, Jo had believed everything he had said. For five months, she had altered the way she spoke, dressed and acted, trying desperately hard to please a man whose slightest frown made her panic. It had been a time of her life that Jo had ironically labelled to herself as a 'learning experience', and what she had learned was that, not only didn't she want to change her personality for a man's pleasure, she simply couldn't. She was Jo, and if another man came into her life, he was going to have to accept her for exactly who she was.

She closed the door behind her as softly as possible, not wanting to wake anyone since it was near midnight, and then crept softly towards the stairs, cursing the yellow alligator that threatened to fall off the top of the pile of animals and pressing her chin to its plush head to keep it steady.

'Home at last.'

The words stopped her cold and she turned slowly towards the den where the door had opened, throwing a slanted rectangle of light down the carpeted hallway and illuminating her face. Jo suddenly felt utterly ridiculous as Conrad's eyes swept over her. The red stetson sat at a precarious angle on her head and she could sense that several feathers hastily stuck in its brim during the evening had come loose and were dangling near her ear, lightly tickling the skin. Her bandana had worked its way around her neck so that the knot no longer was at the front and the bronco imprinted on the fabric was now bucking over her left shoulder. Her purse dangled from one crooked elbow and she had just managed to maintain a grip on the teddy bear's ear with the forefinger and thumb of her right hand. Its body, bulky and pink, kept banging against her knees and tangling with the beaded fringes of her Indian belt.

'I didn't think anyone was up,' she said, clearing her throat.

'Have a nice time?'

'Lovely, thank you.'

Conrad leaned against the doorway, his hands jammed into the pockets of his slacks, his shoulders broad against the wooden frame. Jo could sense a tension in him and wondered if he was offended by her date with Roddy, but his next words seemed careless and unconcerned. 'You seem to have caught Stampede fever.'

Jo gave an uncomfortable laugh. 'Roddy likes games of chance.'

'Did you like the rodeo?'

'Interesting but crazy.' She shifted the teddy bear's ear to her left hand and placed her right one on top of the alligator.

'Crazy?'

'I think anyone who climbs on to a loco horse and gets bounced around until every bone is bruised just to demonstrate perseverance is nuts.'

He shrugged. 'Everyone has some arena where they like to prove their point.'

She tucked the alligator more tightly under her chin, aware that its yellow snout was gaping right in Conrad's direction. 'I guess so.'

'And I'd bet my bottom dollar that yours would be in coal reclamation.'

'You'd win,' she said.

'That's why I thought you might like to go to the mine with me tomorrow.'

'In Crow's Nest?'

'Yup—where I practise plundering and corporate pillage.'

Jo had the grace to blush, but Roddy's request was uppermost in her mind. 'When do we leave and how long will we be staying?'

Conrad's face was too much in shadow for a smile to be evident. 'Overnight and bright and early, New York. I'll see you at seven.'

Jo had a *déjà vu* feeling as they drove along the road that approached Crow's Nest Pass, the peaks of the Seven Sisters looming to the north, the rolling prairie land falling behind. The car went over the divide as it headed west and then passed through coal country, through small towns like Michel and Natal, decaying villages that had been built on the wealth of coal in the 30's and 40's and then left to die slowly when mining went into its slump. There were still old and darkened mine cars on the no longer used rails and boarded up houses made of dull grey and black clapboard that had once been the homes of miners. The newer mines, like that belonging to Wyatt Mining, were further west, and the men who worked those mines now lived in trailer courts where the mobile homes were arranged in the pattern of a small suburb with gravel streets, the occasional tree, laundry hanging out on lines and children riding their bikes and playing on swing sets. The families moved wherever work beckoned, taking out the blocks from underneath their trailers and hooking them on to trucks. It gave them, Jo thought, the feeling that they'd invested in something that was theirs. The old company towns with their company houses had left the miners with nothing they could call their own.

A small town had grown up near the trailer parks, and it boasted several bars and a shopping centre. But there was no library and no movie house and its residents had to drive west to Fernie or east to Blairmore to find entertainment and a greater variety of stores. Of all the passes through the Canadian Rockies, Crow's Nest was probably the least likely to attract tourists and guests. It lacked the dramatic beauty of Jasper and Banff further north where the elevation in the mountains was far greater and the scenery more lovely and panoramic.

Jo and Conrad didn't talk much during their drive from Calgary. He seemed buried in thought and, aside from a few comments, did not engage her in conversation. The car swept through the Pass and then made a turn on to the gravel road that led up to the Wyatt Mining operations. Mining was a round-the-clock business, and the site looked like a hive of activity. Jo could see the trucks going back and forth from the mile-long cut that had been dug into the mountainside, the rumble of their wheels drowning out every other sound and the dust thrown up in their wake so thick that it darkened the horizon with swirling brown clouds.

Conrad pulled up before a set of trailers and, as they got out of the car, the noise and dust became even more pervasive. Jo was glad when Conrad led her into a trailer and closed the door behind them. The quiet inside was soothing.

'Jacques, Bill, Dan, this is Jo Davidson. She's a geologist and interested in coal mining.'

Jo smiled and shook hands with the three men who turned out to be the foreman, the pit manager and the office manager of Wyatt Mining respectively. They were seated around a table sharing coffee and doughnuts and only Dan, the office manager, looked as if he'd spent the morning indoors. Both Jacques and Bill were dressed in heavy boots, socks that were already darkened with coal soot, jeans, khaki shirts made of a heavy, durable cotton and their faces were darker just below the forehead where the lines from the hard hats they had worn were still visible. The office itself, was typical of every mining or geological site that Jo had ever visited or worked on. The furniture was plain and sturdy; there was no decoration except for the inevitable calendar which in this case, to Jo's relief, had a beach scene as opposed to the customary nude pin-up. One wall had shelves crammed with file boxes and piles of papers. She felt very much at home as she sat down, accepted a doughnut and a plastic cup of coffee and listened to the four men talk.

As the absentee owner, Conrad was brought up-to-date on the latest news; reports on coal production, the break-down of machinery, a small incident of vandalism and one reported injury that would require workmen's compensation. When the men were through and both Jacques and Bill had left to go back on site, Conrad signed a few papers for Dan and then indicated Jo with a wave of his hand.

'The lady needs to learn about our flow of money, Dan. Give her a short course on mining economics, will you?'

Dan, tall, thin and reedy, gave Conrad an uncertain glance. 'You mean cost analyses?'

Conrad gave Jo a grin. 'I want her to see what happens when freight costs go up a dollar a ton, Dan. That sort of thing. I'll be back for lunch.'

Within the next two hours, Jo had learned everything she wanted to know about mining costs plus more. It was, she found out, extremely complicated on one level and extremely simple on another. Labour, machinery and freight costs had to be weighed against depreciation allowances, income, assets and investments. The accounting procedures were complex and, while she didn't understand them all, Dan was able to bring information close enough to her uneducated level so that she had a basic grasp of the mechanics of running the mine. But in a way, the economics of it reminded her of household expenses. When meat went up in price, she and Emily had gone on a regimen of semi-vegetarianism. When freight costs went up or the labour union negotiated for better health benefits and the price of coal sank, the same sort of financial squeeze occurred. What Jo hadn't realised was how iffy running the mine actually was in terms of profit. Only recently had it shown any gain; during previous years it had run, quite definitely, in the red.

She expressed her thoughts later to Conrad when, after lunch, he drove her around the site and then led her on a short walking tour. 'I never realised what a fine line you're drawing,' she said, picking her way over some beams on the ground and being thankful that she'd worn her hiking boots, an old pair of jeans and a blouse that had seen better days. Within minutes she could feel the fine black soot working its way down the back of her neck and into the pores of her face. Her head was protected by a hard hat, but her skin, she knew, was going to be black before the afternoon was over.

'Coal mining's been tight for years.'

'And reclamation is expensive.'

'It isn't quite as simple as you thought, is it?'

She shook her head and concentrated on where she was walking. The ground, at this part of the site, was littered with debris; broken boards, pipes and metal beams. Conrad took her arm to help her over a large beam, and she glanced at him quickly, noting how wide his grey eyes seemed beneath the level rim of his miner's hat, the way specks of dark soot had worked their way into his golden moustache and the rivulets of sweat that dripped from his sideburns down the lean side of his jaw. Conrad looked very masculine and very sure of himself out here in the working world where muscle and brawn counted. He wore boots that were darker than hers and well wrinkled from use, thick grey socks, heavy blue jeans and a black T-shirt that clung to the broad muscles of his chest and left his arms bare. He wore a watch on his left wrist, its leather strap wide and brown against his tanned skin.

'What about government grants?' she asked.

'They'd help, of course, but everyone wants a share of government money and it isn't so easy to find. The environmentalists have a hard enough time raising money for research.'

'It's true,' she acknowledged, 'but lots of research has already been done on reclamation. It's there for the asking. All you have to do is implement it.'

'Now, New York,' he chided. 'Admit that a lot of the research is theoretical at best.'

'Some of it hasn't been tested, but that's no reason not to try.'

'But it's costly. One of the big mining concerns further north had a nursery that grew the very trees that one lab considered perfect for reclamation, only to discover that at higher elevations the trees wouldn't take. They had to get seeds from the same type of trees, only ones that grew six thousand feet higher, nurse those along to seedlings and try an implant before they were successful. There was some subtle genetic difference between trees grown below elevation and those above, but the scientists hadn't foreseen the difficulty.'

'It's bound to be hit or miss,' she said. 'It's a new field, after all.'

'I've never had an objection to reclamation, you know. I'm not fighting it, but it takes a lot of persuasion to convince my Board of Directors to release funds for the bulldozing equipment to change the shape of slag heaps so that they'll be sloped properly for drainage, for the foliage that needs to be planted and the care it will require to make sure it grows. The manpower costs are steep.'

Jo could see that; she could already see how much money and investment had been made just to run Wyatt Mining. There were men crawling all over the site and a constant movement of trucks and machinery. The action seemed chaotic and erratic but she knew there was a pattern to it. While they had been walking, a whistle had blown, sending men scurrying away from the pit. The ensuing blast had shaken the earth, as several tons of dynamite had exploded to break the rock off a coal seam. In each direction she could see destruction; trees that had been felled to make way for trucks, earth overturned and gravel laid to replace what had once been forest floor.

'You mean,' she asked, 'that you would begin a project if given some government support?'

'You know, I hate to ruin your concept of me as "the ruthless plunderer", but I already have a project laid out.'

Jo turned to him in surprise, not believing her ears. 'Why didn't you tell me that earlier?' she asked.

'Hell, and ruin all the fun? You're a sight when you're mad, New York.'

'Damn you all . . .' Jo would have gone on further, proving once and for all that she could curse with the best of them, but she'd been so preoccupied by Conrad's words and so busy staring at his grinning profile that she missed a step, tripped over a piece of pipe and fell flat on her face in the dirt.

Conrad was quickly at her side, squatting beside her on his toes, helping her turn over and putting his arm around her shoulders as she sat up. 'You okay?'

'You're not going to believe this,' Jo said, taking a deep shaky breath and leaning against his arm, 'but I think I twisted my ankle.'

Conrad looked down in disbelief at her sturdily booted feet. 'You mean it runs in the family?'

Jo's smile was tremulous at best. 'The weak left ankle syndrome; it's congenital.'

But fortunately, her ankle was merely sprained and

not broken. With Conrad's help, she limped back to the office where Dan clucked with sympathy and got out the first aid kit while Conrad gently took off her boot and sock and manipulated her foot.

'I think you'll live to walk another day, New York.'

'What about today?'

'Nope, you're going to soak this in the coldest water I can find and then we'll bandage it up tight. You're going to have to be an armchair miner for the rest of the day. Dan will keep you occupied with fairy tales about coal barons in quest of ore and dragons dressed up as government regulation agencies. That should keep her amused, don't you think, Dan?'

'Sure thing, Conrad. We've got lots of stories about those.'

Dan made a valiant effort to keep Jo from thinking about her ankle for the next hour and she didn't let it show that his endeavours were in vain, but the pain was sufficient to make her mind stray frequently.

'Would you like some aspirin?' he asked, interrupting himself.

'That would be nice,' she had to admit, smiling at him and liking him more than she had during the morning when he'd been so cut and dry in dealing with financial facts and data. 'Do you live here in Crow's Nest?' she asked as he brought her a glass of water and two pills.

'No, I've got a home in Blairmore. The school there is nice for the kids.'

'You wouldn't want to live in a bigger place? Calgary, for instance.'

Dan rubbed a hand over his thinning brown hair. 'No, I like a small town life and I enjoy working for Conrad. He's got a good operation down here; it's clean and it's efficient.'

Jo remembered Roddy's urgings. 'He said he has a reclamation project on the boards.'

'That's your field, isn't it?' At her nod, he went on. 'His father didn't care about reclamation but then in those days it wasn't an issue. Conrad's seen it coming down the pike for a couple of years now, and he doesn't want to waste the energy fighting it, I guess. His ideas are expensive and ambitious, but with some cooperation from the government and the conservation people it might work. The trouble is that there's always those folks who won't put their money where their mouths are.'

'That's true, I suppose,' Jo murmured. It hadn't occurred to her until now that the very vocal and vociferous reclamation groups were not particularly generous with funds or efforts to fund raise. They tended to look to other groups to finance reclamation ventures—the government, the coal companies themselves. But the job, of course, was an enormous one. It just wasn't Conrad's generation of executives who were responsible for the momentous slag heaps and torn apart landscapes. There were those before them who had been responsible for decisions whose impact could still be felt today.

'Do you want to see it—the reclamation project?'

'I'd love to, is it for this site?'

Dan shook his head. 'An orphan site that Conrad's father abandoned about twelve years ago.' He handed her a thick booklet. 'Conrad had a consultant look at it and draw up some plans.'

The project was written up in a two hundred page document with addendums, appendices and a bibliography. Jo delved into it while Dan turned away to work on some papers, but despite her interest her eyes drooped as she read and she fell into an exhausted sleep, her head tilted back against the chair, her dark hair tumbling against its cracked brown leather, the report open and upside down on her knee. It wasn't until a truck rumbled by and made the thin walls of the trailer shudder that Jo awoke to find Dan gone and Conrad sitting opposite her at the desk, his blond head bent over a mass of papers.

'I ... I'm sorry, I must have dozed off.' She sat up

straighter in the chair and glanced at her watch after noticing that the sun was slanting in the window at an extreme angle. It was already five o'clock.

Conrad looked up from the papers and grinned when he saw Jo's guilty expression and the way she clutched the report to her chest. 'Not the world's most gripping plot, was it?'

Jo gave him a small smile. 'The acting wasn't bad.'

Conrad stood up and stretched, his blond head almost, but not quite, touching the ceiling. 'Give me a slag heap,' he said dryly, 'and I'll give you a star.'

They left not long after that, Jo limping slightly as she walked to the car, her balance aided by Conrad's hand which remained firmly under her elbow. They drove to the motel where they had adjoining rooms, and it was with great relief and satisfaction that Jo stripped off her dirty clothes, unwound the bandage from her ankle and took a long, hot shower, letting the water cascade over her hair and face, washing the black dust out of her skin. When she got out of the shower, she could hear water still running in Conrad's room and, for a second, she allowed her imagination to run full tilt, envisioning with great precision and clarity what it would be like standing next to him, the two of them naked, wet and entwined. Then she took the towel off her head, shook her hair vigorously and concentrated on salvaging her complexion after the day's destruction. It was, she decided firmly, a much safer activity.

They went for dinner to a restaurant whose only claim to culinary excellence was in the glasses of water it served, but neither Conrad nor Jo really noticed the food. They spent the meal arguing the pros and cons of reclamation, the state of mining in general, the provincial economy, political differences between the United States and Canada and the latest elections in both countries. It was the kind of exchange that Jo really enjoyed and rarely participated in—a free and wide-ranging discussion where her views were held, considered and debated in a serious fashion and without any suggestion that because they were a woman's views, they were therefore lesser, biased or ignorant. She found that Conrad had an incisive mind and a highly practical approach to problems. He was admittedly a 'businessman with a business perspective', while Jo saw the world in more idealistic terms, but he didn't laugh or put her opinions down, and she came away from the meal with the good feeling that comes from finding intellectual rapport in pleasant conversation.

It was late by the time that they returned to the motel, and Conrad left Jo at her door, reminding her that they had to be up early next morning to stop at the mine again before heading back to Calgary. She went into her room, got into her nightgown, noticed that her ankle was looking puffier than it had before dinner and decided that she'd better take some aspirin. She was yawning by the time she got into bed, despite her nap, and fell asleep almost immediately, only to wake about two hours later when the throbbing in her ankle had reached such a level of pain that she was tossing and turning, her mind hazy from chaotic dreams of mine sites and rodeos.

Jo switched on her light, sat up in bed and stared at a picture that the motel owners had placed on the wall beside her lamp. It was a poorly rendered mountain scene with a barely recognisable deer standing before a small cabin, and she had the uncharitable thought that it had probably been painted by the owner or one of his relatives. It was certainly indicative of the decor of her room which could only be described as 'tacky tourist'. The bedspread was a beigy-pink with a pattern of bumps in triangles, the walls were a pale blue and the lampshade, to tie it altogether, was pink with a fringe of blue woollen balls.

Thinking about her room, she discovered, was not going to make her ankle go away so Jo stood up, winced at the pain and wandered over to the window where she pulled aside the curtain and stared at the parking lot. There were ten cars and two pickup trucks, their colours indeterminate in the dark. From there, she limped into the bathroom where she took more aspirin and stared at her face in the mirror, noticing how pale she looked, the pallor of her skin set off by the dark mass of her hair, and thinking that she was going to look rotten tomorrow if she didn't get more sleep. She wandered back into the bedroom and sat on the bed, knowing that she shouldn't walk around and wishing that she'd had the foresight to bring along a book to read. She tried sleeping again and when that didn't work, she switched on the light and stared at the ceiling, then at the painting, then at the lampshade and back to the ceiling. By the time her eyes had made the round twice, Jo was thinking of vandalism with a certain amount of malicious pleasure. Defacing the painting might be considered, she thought, a gift to mankind. Too bad she hadn't brought along a knife to . . .

There was a soft knock at her door and she sat up. 'Hello?'

'It's Conrad. Can I come in?'

Jo pulled aside the blanket, thought about the transparentness of her blue nightgown and then shrugged—he'd seen her in it before—and limped over to the door.

'What is it?' she asked as she opened it.

'I saw your light on.' He walked past her and into her room, wearing nothing more than a pair of jeans. The dark-gold hair on his chest gleamed in the lamplight. 'I couldn't sleep either so I thought we might as well join forces. There's not much point in spending the night awake and alone, is there?'

CHAPTER SEVEN

Jo glanced at the straight line of Conrad's back as he walked past her and, shutting the door, said hesitantly, 'I guess not.'

He stood by the bed and looked down at the rumpled sheets and tangle of blankets. 'Is it your ankle?'

'A bit. I just took some more aspirin.'

'Let me look at it.'

Jo sat on the edge of the bed while Conrad knelt before her, his hands probing the swollen flesh. His fingers were gentle and he never pressed hard enough to make Jo even wince, but he knew precisely where the sprain was and he moved her foot from side to side, stopping when she stiffened and shaking his head when he saw how little flexibility her ankle had. Jo watched his hands and then the movements of his head, noticing how tousled his blond hair was and the bronzed width of his shoulders. If she leaned forward, if she just reached out her hand . . .

'You should have let me tape it before dinner,' he said, glancing up at her.

'It felt better then.'

He stood up. 'Off the bed, New York.'

Jo gave him a startled look. 'Why, I . . .'

'I'm going to fix it for you. It's a mess.'

Jo sat in a chair while Conrad tucked the bottom sheet back in, making neat hospital corners, straightened the top sheet and the blanket, folding their upper edges back so that it made a precise hem, and plumped up the two pillows against the headboard. Then he stepped back and surveyed his handiwork. 'Not bad for a bachelor of thirty-seven.'

Jo suppressed a smile. 'This side's uneven,' she said as she pointed to the edge of the blanket.

114

Conrad walked around, stared at it and then said, 'That's okay—that's your side anyway.'

'My side?'

'Are you going to make me sit in that chair?' he asked. 'It looks damned uncomfortable.' His hand went to the belt on his jeans.

'It is,' she conceded, alarmed as he proceeded to unbuckle the belt and zip down his fly, 'but . . .'

'Therefore, I plan to recline on this half of the bed,' Conrad said as he slipped off his jeans, 'while you are entitled to the other half. Unless, of course, you plan to sit up all night.' He was wearing dark blue briefs and he didn't seem to care that Jo was trying to avert her eyes as he lay down on the bed, stretching his long legs out over the spread and crossing his arms across his chest. A triangular pattern of golden hair ran from just below his shoulders to the waistband of his shorts, and darker gold hair gleamed on the muscles of his thighs.

'Who invited you for all night?' she asked incredulously.

'Come on, New York. We've spent the night together before. This isn't a first.'

True, it wasn't a first, but then Jo hadn't expected a second time either. And there was something definitely unsavoury about a motel room, although she was sure that if she pointed *that* out, Conrad would twist the logic around and ask her if she considered co-habiting a sleeping bag as any less unusual and intimate. Short of throwing Conrad out of her room and waking her sleeping neighbours, Jo couldn't see any alternative to climbing into the bed next to him. The chair, straight-backed and upholstered in blue vinyl, was already hurting her back.

She hobbled over to the bed and, for the sake of propriety, climbed under the blanket so that her body would not exactly be touching Conrad's. For a second they sat together, side by side, like two store dummies or a married couple in a situation comedy, and then Conrad started to laugh.

'Shhhh,' she said, laughing too. 'You're going to wake up the people next door. The walls are thin.'

'You're telling me—there's a couple with a kid on the other side of my room and it's been crying on and off since eleven o'clock.'

'That's why you're still up.'

'That's why,' he agreed. He turned over slightly to switch out the light, leaving them in the dark. The curtains were heavy and dark but their ends didn't quite meet, and a thin sliver of light entered the room, fingers of illumination touching the chair, part of the wall, a corner of the bed. The room had a ghostly air as if their faces were touched by moonlight; Jo's a white oval in the mass of dark hair that faded into the shadows, Conrad's angular and planed, his moustache and hair gleaming softly.

He put his arm around Jo's shoulder, pulling her next to him as he sank lower on to the bed so that they were semi-reclining and her body was comfortably enclosed in the curve of his. 'There—nice, isn't it?'

Jo nodded, liking the feel of his arm beneath her neck and the way his hand was massaging her shoulder.

'Now, what are we going to do?' he murmured into her ear.

'Not what you're thinking,' she replied.

'And what's that, mind reader?'

'You know.'

'Nope.'

Jo shifted against him. 'Liar.'

'Yup.'

'Well, not that.'

'Aha—a headache,' he said teasingly.

'I don't sleep with . . .' Jo sought for the right word, 'friends.'

'You prefer enemies?'

'You know what I'm saying.'

'Well, I've heard a little bit about Douglas and he sure as hell sounded like an enemy.'

'I wish Emily hadn't mentioned . . .'

'But she did, New York, and I'd like to know what happened.'

Jo could have refused, but there was something about the soothing, low quality of Conrad's voice by her ear, the warmth of his hand as it caressed her shoulder through the thin fabric of her nightgown, and the fact that she couldn't see his face in the darkness of the room that allowed her to speak. It was almost as if she were confessing, getting the weight of Douglas off her chest, and as if in doing so, she would be free of him forever.

She told Conrad about meeting Douglas Bannock at a party held by a mutual acquaintance who taught physics at the local college. She had, of course, known of Dr Bannock as a well-known geological expert in the study of beach and water formations. Her studies and his overlapped to the extent that they spoke one another's language, and there had been an instant rapport between them that had flattered Jo immensely. Douglas was far older than she—in his mid-forties— divorced, worldly, sophisticated and renowned, and she could hardly believe he was taking an interest in a recently graduated master's degree candidate who had just started teaching and had never published a paper in her life.

His interest, as it turned out, was just as physical as intellectual, and Jo couldn't help succumbing to the enticements he held out before her. There was the attraction of his conversation, the glamour of his company and the admittedly skilled expertise of his lovemaking. He was a good-looking man; tall and greying in a distinguished fashion, and Jo, who had spent her adolescent years studying to the exclusion of romance, was swept off her feet before she even had a chance to sit back, examine the alternatives and decide whether she loved him or not.

'And you slept with him?' Conrad asked.

'Eventually. He was overpowering in a way; he treated me sometimes as if he were a father and I were his daughter.'

'Perhaps,' Conrad said softly, 'you were looking for a father.'

'I . . . I hadn't thought of that,' Jo said slowly, but she saw now that it might be true. She had spent many hours of her childhood and adolescence dreaming about the father she didn't have, and as with all dreams, the vision was greater than any reality could have been. She had wanted a father who would be loving, knowledge-able, handsome and successful, and Douglas had provided all the elements of her dream as if he had, uncannily, read her mind. She had been in awe of him; of his sophistication, his wealth, his house with its paintings and antiques. She had hung on every word that he had spoken, her adoration showing in her eyes. Conrad was right; he had been a father figure to her. With a sudden clarity, Jo understood what her feelings towards Douglas had been—not love, not even infatuation in its normal sense, but an almost childish attachment to a man that she had imbued with the characteristics of the father she wished she had.

And, as if he could read her mind, Conrad asked, 'Did you love him?'

Jo shook her head vehemently. 'I *thought* I loved him. I thought we would be married.'

She told Conrad about the way Douglas had courted her with flowers, mementoes, phone calls and romantic candlelit dinners and that, in her innocence, she had never doubted where the relationship was heading. Douglas might have mentioned marriage in a bantering fashion, but she had taken the thought of it quite seriously. Certainly his ardour alone had convinced her that he was truly in love with her—far more than he'd been with the wife he'd recently divorced or even the one before. He'd explained his marriages to her and Jo, dreamy with infatuation, had believed every word as if it had been the gospel truth.

'I was so naïve,' she said. 'Stupid and naïve.'

'Don't blame yourself,' Conrad said gently, his arm tightening around her. 'You were young and he sounds like the kind of man whose ego required the adoration of young women. I've met the type before.'

'And then one day when he was supposed to pick me up for a party at some friends', he never came. I waited and waited and then I became frantic with worry, thinking that he'd been hurt in a car accident or killed trying to get to my apartment. I even went so far as to call the hospital and police. Finally at Emily's suggestion, I phoned the person having the party and he told me that Douglas had cancelled the day before, saying he was leaving town for a few days.'

'And had he?'

'Yes, the letter came the next day. It was very long and very apologetic and very brutal.' Jo couldn't keep the bitterness out of her voice; she remembered the day that letter had come with horrifying clarity. She'd spent the morning teaching, trying desperately hard not to think of Douglas and not to worry about why he hadn't called her or told her about his plans. She'd come home in the afternoon to find his letter in the mailbox, and there'd been something about the formality of his stationery and his short, blunt script on the envelope that had given her a warning, an omen of what was inside. 'He wrote that he was so sorry to have to break it to me this way, so sorry that he'd misled me. He hadn't meant it to go so far, but I was so lovely and enchanting and all that garbage, that he hadn't been able to bring himself to ... and so forth and so on. The gist was that he was taking a much needed three weeks away in a cottage a friend owned in the Adirondacks, and he was sure that I'd understand that he was really far too old for me and . . .' Her voice broke and Conrad cursed.

'The bastard.'

She took a shaky breath. 'And then during those three weeks, the American Geological Journal came out and there was my research written up under his name. He'd stolen my ideas and my work and written a long think piece on it.' Jo shifted restlessly, remembering her shock on opening the Journal and seeing his name there and then bearing with the knowing looks of her colleagues, who'd been well aware of her research and her love affair. 'I'd talked to him, Conrad, about everything I was doing. He seemed so interested and helpful; he encouraged me to continue. And there was nothing I could do about the stolen material. He was the full professor with all the qualifications. I was nothing more than a lecturer at a community college without a publication to her name. It would have been my word against his authority.' She sighed. 'It wasn't a good time.'

'But why should it have so many repercussions in your life, New York?'

Jo turned slightly and glanced at his face, trying to decipher his expression in the dark. 'Wouldn't it have bothered you?' she asked. 'Wouldn't something like that affect you?'

She felt his shrug. 'I'd chalk it up to experience and keep my mouth shut about my research.'

'But what about how I felt? I believed in him; I thought he loved me.'

'People get what they want,' he said.

'You mean—I wanted him to love me so I believed it?'

'Something like that.'

Jo sat up, moving slightly out of the curve of his arm. 'That's an awfully simplistic philosophy,' she said.

'I told you—I don't go for complicated jargon and pretty theories. I prefer to see things in elemental terms.' When she didn't answer, he went on, 'Look at Emily and Paul, for instance.'

'All right,' she said with a touch of anger. 'Let's look at them. They want to get married.'

'And that makes you mad?'

'Shouldn't it? They don't know one another. They haven't a clue about married life. They're asking for trouble.'

Conrad pulled her firmly back into his arms. 'Take it easy, New York, you're about to take a curve too fast.'

'But you agree with me, don't you? You said Paul shouldn't get married now; he has too much schooling ahead of him.'

'Marriage doesn't make a lot of sense for them in practical terms, but in emotional ones, it does. Paul needs a woman in his life. His mother, to all intents and purposes, abandoned him on my doorstep and he's craved female affection ever since. And Emily's wants are the same; she's lived in a family of women and her hormones are crying out for a man.'

Jo had never thought about Emily in exactly those terms; she'd never thought of her loosely woven relationship with Prudence and the tight weave of her connection to Emily as being a 'family of women'. 'You know they're sleeping together?'

'I figured that one out about two weeks ago.' There was a smile in his voice. 'I almost congratulated Paul and Emily on dexterity; their casts must have required a fair amount of athletic ability.'

'I thought Paul was just fooling around with Emily. I never suspected that they'd consider marriage.'

'And now you can't decide which is worse?'

'I want Emily to get away from here and put some distance between herself and Paul. I want her to *think* about what she's doing.'

'There's not much chance of that,' Conrad said. 'When I left, Paul mentioned something about blood tests.'

Jo twisted right out of his arm. 'You mean they're going for blood tests now!'

'That's the way it looks.'

'But they can't . . . they just can't!'

'Why not?'

Jo pulled herself upright, her arms across her chest in a tight grip as if she could hold in the frantic beating of her heart. 'You encouraged Paul, didn't you?'

'The trouble with you, New York, is that you don't trust a soul,' Conrad said sarcastically. 'Of course, I didn't encourage him. We had a man-to-man talk, and I told him he was plain loco.'

'When do they plan to get married?'

'As soon as the blood tests are in.'

There was a moment of silence while Jo absorbed Conrad's words. Emily had only talked to her about marriage as if it were theoretical, not something they were going to act upon immediately. Jo had thought that she had time to change Emily's mind, to persuade her that a hasty marriage would be folly and to convince her to return to Fairfax before she made a final commitment, but now she realised that Emily wasn't going to give her the chance. Jo clasped her hands together and tried to think of a way of stopping Emily, but there was nothing she could do . . .

'There's not enough time to plan a wedding,' she said lamely.

'I don't think they care.'

Whatever had happened to Emily's dream of a white wedding with bridesmaids and flower girls and . . . 'But what about Prudence?'

'Your mother? From what I gather, Emily doesn't want her to come.'

Jo couldn't blame her, not really. The thought of Prudence in the Wyatt home was enough to even make her flinch. It wasn't as if their mother wasn't presentable or acceptable by most standards. It was just that, if she were honest, Jo would have to admit that Prudence was a bit dotty. Harmless, but dotty. She'd be disorientated by the change of scenery and confused by the new cast of characters. She'd be upset at the idea of Emily's marriage and the fact that she wouldn't be living in New York any more. Jo couldn't blame Emily for wanting to present Prudence with a *fait accompli*. Their life, she knew, would be much easier that way.

'There must be something we can do,' she said.

His voice, when it came, was casual, almost disembodied. 'Why don't you want your sister to be happy, New York?'

Jo was startled. 'I do want her to be happy.'

'Then why are you trying to stop the marriage.'

'Because . . . because it's doomed, that's why. They haven't had enough time to learn about one another, to . . .'

'It's what she wants.'

'She's too young to *know* what she wants.'

'She's only four years younger than you are.'

'But Emily isn't experienced, she doesn't know about . . .'

'I think you're jealous, New York. That's what I think.'

The words hung in the darkness between them until the sound of a truck engine revving up outside broke the silence and the intense grip of Jo's sudden anger. 'How dare you,' she said in a low, trembling voice. 'How dare you imply that I would stand in the way of Emily's happiness and how dare you suggest that I am jealous of someone that I love so dearly . . .'

His hands came out and gripped her shoulders. 'I dare because it's true. It's been written all over your face for weeks. You can't stand the fact that your sister has a lover and is happy for the first time in her life. You can't stand the idea that her lover is actually going to marry her and not abandon her the way Douglas abandoned you. You're so damned jealous that you can't even admit that Paul and Emily are really and truly in love with one another.'

'Leave my room!'

His hands tightened on her shoulders. 'The hell I will. It's about time you listened to the truth.'

'I hate you Conrad,' she hissed.

'You don't hate me at all.'

Jo flung her hair back out of her eyes. 'And now, I suppose, you're going to turn macho on me and tell me how much I'm dying to have you make love to me as if I couldn't resist your . . . your body.'

'Can you?' he asked in a low voice.

'Yes!'

'Can you, Jo?' This time his words were a whisper,

the hands on her shoulders so gentle that she didn't realise he was bringing himself closer to her until he was there, his lips at her mouth, one arm slipping down her back to enfold her waist, his body pressing against hers.

This time he didn't merely brush his mouth against hers; it was a firmer touch, a movement that caught her by surprise so that her mouth parted automatically beneath his. His tongue licked at the corner of her bottom lip and then ran slowly along its edge, a tantalising, teasing stroke that made Jo catch her breath.

'You like that?' he said softly.

'I . . .'

He bent his head and took her mouth with a sudden passion, his tongue meeting hers, entwining and then separating as their lips moved in a sensual union. Jo lost track of everything except the sensations between them; the hard muscles of his chest, the swell of her breasts pressed upwards as he pulled her tighter, the soft bristly feel of his moustache, the curve of his upper arm as she tentatively reached out and touched him—and then the thick, springing feel of his hair in her fingers, short at the back of his neck and longer as she moved her hand upwards.

Conrad lowered her gently to the bed so that they were lying alongside one another, his mouth not moving from hers, his hand sliding up from her waist to the curve of her breast and then cupping the mound of it through her nightgown. Her nipple rose to the demands of his fingers, swelling to a hard point beneath the stroke of his thumb. Jo arched to be closer to him, feeling the hard length of him against her stomach and knowing that her need matched his, knowing that she wanted to yield, knowing that nothing would be so easy as to just say nothing and let his hands complete their work, bringing her to the satiation her body demanded . . .

'No,' she said.

His hand rested on her breast as his head lifted, his

eyes dark in the pale oval of his face. 'Why not?' he replied, his voice rough.

'I . . . I don't want to.'

'Why the hell can't you admit what you want, Jo? Why do you have to camouflage every honest feeling and desire that you want?'

'It's too complicated.'

'It's not complicated at all—Douglas still has power over you.'

'I don't love him! I told you that.'

'I'm not talking about love,' Conrad said with disgust. 'I'm talking about the way you've allowed him to colour your perceptions and change your behaviour. He's left you with an inability to enjoy sex that's crippling.'

'It's not that simple.'

She could feel Conrad shake his head in frustration. 'We like one another; we want one another. There's no one out there judging you. This is strictly between us.'

'I have to judge myself.'

'Against what standard?'

'You wouldn't understand.'

'Damn it, New York, try me.'

Jo turned her head on the pillow and stared into the darkness. 'I'm sorry,' she said.

He let go of her then, and she felt the bed shift as he got off. She sat frozen to her place, listening to the rustlings as he leaned over and picked his jeans up off the floor. She only started to move at the metallic sound of a zipper and the clank of a belt buckle, but by the time she had slid over to the other side of the bed so that she could switch on the light, Conrad was out of the door. The sudden glare of the lamp showed her only the closing door, the utter dreariness of the room and the imprint of his body on the pillow he had been leaning against.

Without realising what she was doing, Jo picked up the pillow and rested her cheek on it, closing her eyes as she did so and smelling a faint hint of the cologne

Conrad had put on after his shower. It had a woody scent, and it filled her with a depth of longing and sadness she had never felt before. Why couldn't she sleep with Conrad? Why had she stopped him like that, ending what would have been pleasurable and satisfying for both of them? She wan't any different from any other woman; her sexual urges were healthy, strong and clamouring for a man's embrace.

Jo pressed the pillow closer to her and clenched her eyes shut in despair. She hated the part of herself that held back, using anger as a barrier to keep Conrad at arm's length, and with all her heart she wished that she could be like Emily. Yes, she was jealous, but not of her sister's happiness or of Paul's commitment. Jo was sick with envy at the joy with which her sister embraced life. Emily had no apprehension, no fear of the future, no sense of danger ahead—she simply moved towards it with the innocent happiness of a young child who runs smiling into the sea, ignorant of the perils beneath its sparkling blue-green surface.

They were exceedingly polite to one another the next day. Breakfast was a formal occasion with enquiries into the state of her foot, the length of time she had slept and 'would you like some more coffee?' and 'please, pass the salt, thank you'. Conrad insisted on holding her arm when they walked to the car, and he treated her like fragile china when they reached the mine. He didn't invite her to go on to the site with him, but suggested that she stay in the trailer until he was done. Jo, in turn, was careful to let Conrad know that she wanted to complete reading his reclamation paper and that she really had no desire to interfere with his day. They drove back to Calgary at noon with the car radio playing continuously so that there would be no need for conversation. Jo understood that Conrad was just as willing as she was to concede that their relationship had come to a dead end. He wanted a woman who would explore the realms of intimacy in the hopes that a friendship would develop, while she preferred the reverse. It was, perhaps, just a matter of style.

Still, Jo ached with a sense of having lost something precious as if she'd given away a jewel of considerable expense, and she couldn't help glancing at him every once in a while and wondering if he felt the same way. She knew that they had many things in common beside a physical attraction for one another. They operated in a similar world; they had language and interests in common. She respected the way his mind worked; she liked the way he attacked a problem, coming at it from every logical angle and then making a clear and rational decision. He had a way of cutting through the verbiage and emotional tangle that accompanied decision-making and, once he'd got to the heart of a problem and determined a solution, he wasn't the sort to waffle or change his mind or agonise about it. There were some ways in which Conrad was exactly as he billed himself—a simple man with no tolerance for frills.

But Jo also couldn't help feeling that his relationships with women were more complex than he admitted. Handling a woman wasn't as easy as tackling a debit sheet or analysing a labour situation, and the fact that Marion was still writing to him, despite Paul's assertion that her letters were only indicative of persistence, suggested to her that Conrad had got himself in a little deeper than was customary. Diane Beauchamp had already hinted at a strong emotional entanglement, and Jo was of the opinion that Conrad's heart wasn't as free as he made it out to be. It was that belief, partially, that had kept her from sleeping with him in the motel.

Jo didn't have any proof that Conrad even cared about Marion, but she was cautious all the same. She didn't want a physical intimacy with a man whose thoughts were turning to another woman. If sleeping with Douglas had taught her anything, it was that a man can use a woman for a number of selfish reasons, not one of which involves the woman's happiness. She

didn't want to think of herself as being an outlet for
Conrad's highly-charged hormonal level or as a passing
sexual partner in a moment of loneliness or as an
obstinate challenge that defied victory. What Jo
wanted was love, but it wasn't a want that she
articulated very often, even to herself. That would have
been admitting a weakness and, as an independent
woman, Jo preferred to think of herself as self-
sufficient. She didn't need a man to supply her with
food, shelter or company, and she wasn't accustomed to
looking deeper or analysing her emotional needs. Love
was merely a luxury item, nice if you could find it and
afford it, but not necessary to her existence.

They arrived at the Wyatt house in mid-afternoon to
find that Emily had got a new cast, shorter and far
more manageable, and that the house was buzzing with
activity. Emily and Paul had decided to get married on
the following Tuesday evening and were planning a
party as a celebration. The fact that they were
labouring under last-minute types of arrangements
didn't seem to bother them in the least. If anything, it
made the wedding that much more exciting. They'd
found a minister, a church, a caterer and an apartment.
Emily was virtually pink with excitement as she regaled
Jo with details of the place she and Paul had found to
live in. It was 'adorable, charming and so cute' with two
bedrooms, a kitchen that was no bigger than a closet
and a fireplace, and it was situated close to the
university. It was also partially furnished so that they
wouldn't have to go out and buy a lot of furniture.

'And Paul has lots of his own stuff,' Emily said that
night, sitting in a chair, as Jo got ready for bed. She
could now hobble around on her own without crutches,
using a cane or any piece of furniture that was handy.
Jo could see that the coming wedding and being mobile
again had given Emily a new lease on life; she had an
aura of vivacity that Jo had never seen before—her eyes
sparkled, her voice had a musical lilt, her small hands

drew pictures in the air. 'All the furniture in the bedroom is his and there's stuff that belongs to his mother in the basement.'

'How nice,' Jo replied as she hobbled over to the closet, hung up a blouse and then hobbled back to the bed where she picked up a pair of jeans.

Emily watched her and then said, 'I can't believe you hurt your ankle—and it's the left one, too.'

'It'll be all right in a day or two.'

'Did you have fun with Conrad?'

'It was a very interesting trip.'

'Really, Jo, you and Conrad have so much in common that it seems a shame that . . .'

'Em, you're barking up the wrong tree.'

'It would just be heavenly if both you and Conrad and Paul and myself were couples. Think of it, Jo. We would be living in the same town, seeing each other all the time, babysitting each other's children . . .'

'Emily!' Jo couldn't help the angry intensity of her voice. 'Stop building unrealistic castles in the air. It's . . . adolescent.'

'I guess you always were the pragmatic one,' Emily said with resignation, 'and I was the dreamer.'

Jo picked up her jeans and folded them. 'Always,' she said dryly.

But Emily was already discussing kitchen appliances, and Jo suddenly understood how very close this marriage to Paul approximated her sister's dreams. She'd never realised that Emily was so traditional and so desirous of a husband and a family. She had thought, she saw now with sadness, that she and Emily were the same and had the same ambitions and desires, never perceiving that beneath her sister's amiability and docility was a mind that was quite intent upon its own path. All it had taken was Paul to activate those dreams and put the stars into Emily's eyes.

Her sister had now gone from the subject of kitchenware to her job. 'And Paul says that if it's too late for me to get a teaching job that I can work at the

Registrar's Office at the University. He knows the woman who's in charge of personnel. If I worked there we wouldn't need an extra car.'

'What about your job back home?'

'Oh, I called Carson and told him that I wouldn't be coming back. He expressed the usual regrets, but he won't have any trouble getting someone else. Lots of people are looking for teaching jobs.'

'What are you going to do about Prudence?'

'Oh, well . . .' Emily had the grace to look guilty. 'Paul and I have decided that we'll fly east at Christmas.'

'And who's going to tell her about the wedding?'

'I thought . . . well, it seemed best to me . . .'

Jo turned to her with a knowing look. 'You want me to be the bearer of bad news.'

Emily spread out her hands in a gesture of entreaty. 'You're so much better at handling her, Jo, and she'll take it better from you.'

'She's going to be unhappy about it.'

Emily's mouth took on a stubborn line. 'I can't live my life for Prudence.'

'You could have waited,' Jo said in a reasonable tone. 'You could have gone back to Fairfax with me and had the wedding there. You can still change your mind if you want to.'

'But I don't! Oh, Jo, will you do it for me? Please?'

Jo opened a drawer and placed the jeans inside. 'Of course, I'll do it. I'd rather Prudence learned about it from me than in a letter.'

There was silence for a moment and then she heard Emily get up off the chair and walk towards her. Jo deliberately didn't turn around to face her sister, but kept her back turned, her hands moving in the drawer as if she were busy, not wanting Emily to see the despair and unhappiness written in her eyes. But she felt Emily's arms come around her waist and could feel her sister's cheek pressed against her back. A lump rose in her throat at that familiar childish hug.

'Oh, Jo, be happy for me, please.'

Jo kept her face averted. 'I'll try.'

'Because it's so wonderful and I love Paul so much. It will work out; you'll see—it really will. I've never wanted anything in my life as much as I've wanted to marry Paul. And he wants it to. It's like a dream coming true, Jo. My own personal prayer to God coming true—just for me.'

CHAPTER EIGHT

THE week before the wedding was one of the hardest Jo ever had to live through. There were private discussions, family conferences, a thousand phone calls to be made and a shopping list a mile long. The speed with which Emily and Paul had decided to be married meant that neither Paul's mother nor Conrad's father would be able to attend the wedding. They were both vacationing in Europe, and it was decided that they shouldn't even be sent invitations—there was no point putting pressure on them to return.

'And I'm not even sure,' Paul said, 'that my mother would come anyway.'

They were sitting at the table in the breakfast nook, and Jo glanced uncertainly at Conrad to see how he would take this hint of his half-sister's defection. 'She might not,' he agreed dryly. 'Mona isn't known for having altruistic motives.'

'You mean—she wouldn't want to come to her son's wedding?' Jo ventured.

Conrad shrugged. 'Not if she's busy with something else—that's the way Mona is and has been. She was spoiled rotten as a child and is firmly convinced that the world owes her a living. I can't say it's her fault because her mother never denied her a thing; she grew up believing that she should always have her own way.'

With that, the discussion of the Wyatt family was over, but not before it had come home to Jo very strongly that the Wyatt family despite their wealth, was, in some ways, not so different from her own—they had suffered, she thought, from the same sort of emotional deprivation. Conrad's mother had died when he was small and, at that time, Mona who was twelve years older than Conrad had been sent to private finishing schools in Switzerland. It had been a household of men only for many years; first Conrad and his father and then Conrad and Paul. They'd had Mrs Beattie, of course, but Jo didn't think that even the kindness of a housekeeper was the same as a loving wife or mother or daughter. Just as she and Emily had been brought up without any male influence, so had Conrad and Paul missed out on the softening influence of women. Perhaps that's why Conrad's approach to her had been so blunt and direct; perhaps he didn't know that some women required a more oblique statement of sexual attraction, one that was less threatening and frightening.

Not that there was even the slightest hint of physical attraction any more, of course. Conrad made it painfully clear that his interest in Jo had subsided completely. They rarely talked and, when they met, the exchange was brief, cold and formal. He was charming and sweet to Emily which made the contrast all the harder to bear, and Jo occasionally caught Paul watching her as if he wondered what had gone on between the two of them on their trip to Crow's Nest Pass. Jo suffered a lot more than she would have thought possible from Conrad's aloofness. She liked talking to him; she enjoyed having him around her; she missed the sensation of aliveness he brought to her with his physical presence alone. When Conrad was nearby, her heart beat more strongly, colours seemed more vibrant and the air seemed to shimmer with a suppressed excitement. When he was gone the world seemed to flatten and become dull, and she found herself wandering around the house or its grounds, her path aimless, her mind drifting like a leaf caught in the meandering, erratic course of a creek or river.

It was at this time, when her ankle had healed, that Jo decided to ignore Big John's dislike of women and learn how to ride. When she approached him, the little man grumbled and swore under his breath, but he did as she asked, bridling up a horse that he described as 'fifteen years old and so gentle she wouldn't step on a fly'. Jo followed his bow-legged stride out to the corral where he taught her how to climb on and gave her some rudimentary instructions on how to make 'Noodle' turn left and right.

'Noodle?' Jo asked.

'She was once the most addle-pated hoss around,' Big John mumbled between chomps of his cigar, 'but she calmed down with old age. Now, don't go gettin' fancy on her; she ain't the brightest thing between the ears.'

'I won't,' Jo promised.

'And talk to her a bit as you go or she forgets what she's about.'

It was the understatement of the year, Jo discovered, because Noodle was interested in everything in the corral except what Jo wanted her to do. She liked to stop at fence posts and stare off into the sunset. She liked to munch the high grass that grew at one corner of the corral, the tops poking through the fence. She liked to sidle over to the fence gate and rub up against the bolt. What she didn't much like doing was walking in a continuous circle with a rider on her back and Jo, who didn't have the nerve to do anything more than talk as Big John had suggested, spoke sweet words of encouragement into Noodle's roan-coloured ear.

'Come on, Noodle, move it.'

'That was left, Noodle. I pulled the left rein which means you go left.'

'You know something, Noodle? You have the perfect retirement policy—slow down to the point that they give up making you go.'

In a few days and with a great deal of relief on Jo's part, Big John decided to graduate her from Noodle to a small white mare called Fleet of Foot which he swore was the most docile thing in the barn.

'Than why is she called Fleet of Foot?'

'We was bein' sarcastic,' he answered her, pulling back his stetson and wiping his forehead with a huge handkerchief. He was a man whose skin was leathery from the sun, whose nose was large and red and whose face was so round he looked as if he had swallowed the moon. Paul vowed that Big John had once been married, but his wife had left him because the only thing he truly loved was horseflesh.

'You mean she should have been named Slow as Molasses?'

It was the first time Jo had even gotten a smile out of Big John. 'Yeah,' he said, 'somethin' like that.'

Fleet of Foot was used to being ridden around the property and, as promised, she was calm without being so easily distracted the way Noodle had been. Jo took her on a path nearby the fence that lined the Wyatt lands and, going at a slow walk, enjoyed the creaking sound of the saddle in the quiet of the prairie, the way she and the horse cast long shadows on the ground and the feeling she had of being one with nature; the earth, the sky and the long, angled grasses. It was only when she was riding and away from the house that Jo felt her tensions subside and the unhappiness within her ease. For a couple of hours a day she was able to forget that Emily was about to be married and that she was still living in a house with a man who treated her with polite indifference.

She was riding near on the eastern section of the property late one afternoon when she felt Fleet of Foot suddenly get restless, turning her head from side to side, her white ears pricked forward.

'What is it, girl?' Jo asked, but then she heard the sound of hooves behind her and turned the mare around, knowing who was coming and trying to prepare herself for the encounter.

As Conrad rode up to her, the sun at his back threw a dark, elongated shadow in front of his horse's legs. That shadow plus the drumming sound of the horse's hooves on the hard earth brought back to Jo, in an eerie sort of way, the memory of her dream many nights before and, despite the heat of the sun on her head, she found herself shivering and clutched the reins tightly in her hands as if the narrow leather straps could give her strength. Conrad was riding a big golden stallion, a fierce animal that stood hands higher than Jo's mare. She could feel Fleet of Foot pull on the bit slightly as rider and stallion approached, and she sympathised with the mare's nervousness. There was something about Conrad's control of the horse, his hands gripping the reins, his thighs tight on the saddle, that made Jo's throat go dry.

'So you've taken up riding,' Conrad said, pulling beside her and looking at her with eyes that were shaded by his stetson. Like Jo, he was wearing a plaid shirt, jeans and blunt-toed boots.

'I like it.'

'Fleet's a good mount for a beginner.'

'I started on Noodle actually.'

'That's Big John's strategy—if a rider doesn't have patience with Noodle, he won't let them ride anything else.'

'Frankly, I think Noodle is senile.'

Conrad smiled. 'So do I.'

Fleet of Foot shied away suddenly from the stallion and Jo, startled, grabbed the pommel of the saddle as she felt herself starting to slip. Conrad leaned over and grabbed the mare's bridle to steady her. 'You don't much like Golden Boy, do you, Fleet?'

The mare gave a soft whinny as if she were in agreement and Jo said, 'He's a big horse.'

Since the mare had stopped moving, Conrad let go of her bridle and pulled tightly on Golden Boy who had taken it into his head to paw the ground and throw his head from side to side. For a second both horse and rider seemed to be locked into a battle, but then the stallion relaxed and Conrad looked up at Jo, saying, 'Emily sent me out here. She seems to need the advice of a fashion consultant and neither Paul nor I fit the bill.'

Jo sighed and obediently turned the mare around so that she pointed in the direction of the house. 'I can't wait,' she said with distaste, 'until the wedding is over.'

'You're not enjoying it much, are you?' Jo shook her head as Fleet of Foot settled into a comfortable walk. Conrad brought the stallion into stride beside her. 'Are you heading back home once it's over?'

Jo glanced at him quickly and then back to a spot between the mare's ears. 'Yes, I thought I'd go the next day. School begins in a couple of weeks and I have a lot to do.'

'How many courses do you teach?'

'Three—two general geology classes and one on glacial geology.'

'Do you have a lot of students?'

Jo saw that it was going to be a very polite conversation. They would discuss her work, perhaps his work, and never touch on the subject that rested so uneasily between them. She tried to make Fleet of Foot go a little bit faster, but either she wasn't very skilful at sending messages or the mare was simply not interested, because she continued quite sedately on, no longer seeming to care that the stallion was walking alongside of her.

'Yes,' she said coldly.

'Well, if you want to stay longer, you can.'

Jo noted the casualness of the invitation and Conrad's obvious uninterest in her answer. He was leaning forward and patting Golden Boy on the neck, murmuring something to him.

'I don't see any point in that . . . do you?'

Conrad sat up, looked at her, his gaze level and steel-grey. 'No,' he said with an indifference that equalled hers. 'I suppose I don't.'

On the day of the wedding, Paul swore that all the planets were in conjunction and the auspices were favourable for the marriage. It was a beautiful, bright and sunny day with hardly a breath of wind to disturb Emily's carefully curled hair or blow away the cloths that had been placed on the two long tables on the patio that would feed the guests. The ceremony went off without a hitch, and everyone laughingly commented to the bride on the way in which her new white cast so perfectly matched the white of her dress. Emily went up the aisle on Conrad's arm and down on Paul's, and she managed both journeys with a minimum of hobbling and awkward stops and starts. She wore a dress that she and Jo had found after scouring the city, a delicate white shirtwaister with a lace collar and cuffs. They had decided against a veil and gone for flowers instead, small blue and white blossoms that were tucked into the blonde curls and braids that a hairdresser had so ingeniously designed for the wedding.

Paul looked handsome in a dark blue suit, his dark hair slicked back and his elbow in an elegant silk blue sling. The cast and sling were a cause of many jokes and quips, none of which amused Jo, but had everyone roaring with laughter. Conrad also wore a blue suit and the sight of his blond head bent over Emily's as he presented her to Paul before the altar made a catch come into Jo's throat. She watched Paul put the ring on Emily's finger, the gentle kiss that he gave her and then Emily's tremulous smile as she turned to walk back up the aisle. Despite the last minute arrangements and the simplicity of the service, the wedding was really quite lovely and no one could miss the obvious feeling of love that existed between the bride and the groom. Jo could feel tears, unwanted and unbidden rising to her eyes, and she didn't join in with the well-wishers at the front of the church, who were congratulating Paul and kissing a smiling Emily. She slipped into her car and drove back to the house, her mind firmly on the coming party and thinking that someone in addition to Mrs Beattie should be checking on the caterers.

But everything was under Mrs Beattie's competent control and Jo wandered to her room where she stared at her reflection in the mirror, wondering how her face could appear so calm. She smiled experimentally and than ran her fingers through her black hair. She'd had it trimmed so it fell in different lengths around her face and curled on to her shoulders. It was a shaggy look that suited her and her lifestyle; quick, casual and busy. The dress she had chosen for the wedding was one that she thought she could wear again. It was a cream silk with a high collar and a bodice that buttoned to one side, a wide sash and a flowing skirt. She wore bone high-heeled sandals to match and a broad-brimmed bone hat decorated with pale blue feathers. Paul had paid for Emily's dress, but Jo had insisted on paying for her own, although she could dearly afford it. Now that Emily would no longer be contributing to the rent, her salary was going to be strained to the limit.

She had never thought to see Emily married, had never thought she would be living alone without her sister for company. She hadn't shown much foresight, Jo realised as she turned away from the mirror, but then life can play tricks, dirty nasty tricks on your expectations. She had no desire to return to Fairfax where an empty apartment awaited her and, for the first time, the thought of school and her students and her research didn't give her a lift. Life stretched out bleakly before her—a monotonous landscape of work and more work. She'd never been good at leisure; Emily was the one who liked to go to the movies and think up dinner parties. She had often interrupted Jo in the middle of marking papers or planning a project to insist that they have a game of tennis or go shopping or drop in on friends and, as Jo walked down the stairs to join the wedding guests, she had her first inkling of the true dimensions of the rift Emily's absence would make in her life. It would be far greater than losing a rent sharer or a dinner companion. It was going to hurt, Jo understood, for a long, long time.

Perhaps the sadness of her thoughts remained in her eyes or could be seen in her expression, because Roddy commented to her later, 'It's hard to see Emily go, isn't it?'

Jo turned to him. 'Yes, it is.' They were standing on the Wyatts' patio, drinking cocktails while a group of people swirled around them, the air filled with laughter, conversation and the tinkling sound of glasses being picked up and put down on trays as waiters moved smoothly in the throng.

'You were close to your sister?' Maria asked. His fiancée was exactly as Roddy had portrayed her—tall, blonde, not beautiful in any classical sense, but attractive with a mobile mouth and a lovely smile. She and Roddy were almost the same height, and she frequently gave him a level look as if to say, 'Come off it, Roddy, I've heard that before'. Her attitude, Jo saw, kept Roddy on his toes, his demeanour toned down and his activities a bit less frenetic.

'We shared an apartment at home,' Jo told her.

'I always wanted a sister,' Maria said mournfully. 'Four brothers is what I got and they made my life a misery.'

Roddy grinned at Jo. 'She was a tomboy—that's why she went into geology.'

Maria shrugged eloquently and then sipped at her champagne. 'What else could I do?'

'Speaking of which,' Roddy said, drawing closer to Jo, 'did you talk to Conrad about starting a reclamation project?'

'He beat me to it—he's already thinking about one.'

Roddy drew back. 'No kidding!'

'No kidding.'

'Hey, that's great news!'

Maria gave Jo an amused look. 'Roddy is turned on by reclamation projects.'

Roddy put his arm around her. 'Jealous, sweetheart?'

Maria's voice was affectionate. 'How would *you* like to play second fiddle to a slag heap?'

There were toasts after that; several funny ones from friends of Paul who thought the fact that the couple were honeymooning in their apartment was worth several embarrassing comments that brought blushes to Emily's cheeks, and a serious one from Conrad who welcomed Emily into the Wyatt family with considerable charm and warmth. Dinner was a sit-down affair with food that was unpretentious but good; prime rib roast, corn on the cob, potato salad and a tall wedding cake with fruitcake inside the white icing.

Jo sat at Conrad's right with Diane Beauchamp at his left and Frank next to her. For a while the conversation revolved around the latest city scandal and a proposed strike by bus drivers but Diane, noting the way Jo picked at her food, brought the talk back to a personal level.

'This isn't the happiest occasion for you, is it?' she asked with sympathy in her voice.

Jo could feel Conrad's eyes on her profile. 'I'm going to miss Emily, of course. We are . . . were very close.'

Diane threw Conrad a mischevious look. 'You know, Con, there's ways of remedying the situation.'

'Are there?' he drawled.

Frank put down his fork. 'Now, Diane,' he admonished, 'leave poor Conrad alone. You've been trying to matchmake for the last five years and your record is abysmal.'

'But look how simple it would be,' she replied, tilting her blonde head and giving Jo and then Conrad appraising looks. 'Two sisters just falling on the Wyatt doorstep; Con and Paul both looking for wives . . .'

Jo could feel the hot blush rising in her cheeks and she looked down at her plate while Conrad spoke.

'I didn't know I was looking for a wife.'

Diane's teasing voice went on. 'You're going to be a grouchy old bachelor, set in your ways and wretched, if you don't watch out.'

Frank leaned over and said to Conrad in a conspiratorial voice, 'Married women hate bachelors—it's threatening. They're afraid their husbands will get ideas.'

Conrad grinned at Diane. 'Now, why would I need a wife when I can get all I want just by . . .'

Diane waved a scolding finger at him. 'I do not want

to hear tales about your degenerate single life. Every article I've ever read about bachelors says that they're the world's most unhappy men. They're unsettled, lonely and miserable.'

'You don't believe everything you read, do you, Diane?'

'Bachelors have an extremely high suicide rate, Conrad. Just think what you're risking by not throwing yourself into wedded bliss.'

Frank raised his eyebrows. 'Bliss?'

'Bliss,' Diane said firmly.

'Come on, Diane. I don't look unhappy, do I?'

'I think single life must be hell, frankly. I wouldn't know what to do if I didn't have Frank to nag. I'd be bored, lonely, unhappy . . .'

Frank interjected, 'The key word is nag, Conrad. Don't forget it.'

Diane turned to Jo. 'You're single,' she said. 'Wouldn't you rather be married?'

It was a tense moment suddenly. Jo could feel Conrad's silence beside her, his full attention on the words she was about to utter. Diane seemed to notice the tension, her blue eyes darting between them as if she had caught a whiff of a bit of extremely juicy gossip. Frank seemed oblivious to it all as he speared a large piece of cake.

'That's a leading question,' he said. 'Don't answer, Jo. You don't have to incriminate yourself.'

'No,' Jo said, 'I don't mind answering. The truth is . . .' What was the truth? she suddenly wondered. A month ago she would have answered that no, she never wanted to be married, that she couldn't think of one single reason why she should be, and that she was independent enough to take care of herself, but now the response seemed pat and shallow as if she were mouthing words from an angry feminist text. Yet, she couldn't be truthful because she no longer knew exactly what the truth was, so she changed what she had been about to say, her words evasive, 'There have been times in my life when I might have preferred marriage and other times when being single seemed a better way to live.'

Conrad leaned forward, his grey eyes on her face, watching it carefully. 'And right now?' he asked, his voice seemingly casual as if to mislead their audience.

Jo looked at him directly, allowing a small smile to curve her lips, a careless, throw-away sort of smile, the kind she might bestow on any man who was asking her a provocative, flirtatious question. 'Oh, I'm anti-marriage right now, and one wedding in the family is enough, don't you think? Otherwise we might overdose on sloppy sentimentality.' She turned and looked at the Beauchamps, her smile deepening. 'And get fat on fruitcake.'

The wedding party seemed to go on endlessly. When the meal was over, Paul turned his stereo and record collection over to a friend and the guests started dancing. The patio was lit by bobbing coloured lights that threw greens, blues and pinks over the cement walks and tinged faces and hands with light, pastel shades. People were gathered in small groups near the bar and the music drowned out the sounds of their conversations, but Jo could see their mouths smiling, their hands making animated gestures.

Emily was in the centre of such a throng, surrounded by Paul's friends, her face gleaming and happy. The flowers had come down from her hair and several curls loosened to hang on her neck and at her temples. Paul had his good arm around her, and they often looked at one another with secret, meaningful smiles. At that moment, they seemed quite solitary despite the crowd around them, two lovers sharing a moment, a message, an understanding. Jo kept away from them, wandering often into the kitchen to help Mrs Beattie, who would shoo her out, telling her to have a good time, and occasionally talking to the guests. She felt out-of-place and awkward, knowing that she didn't fit into the celebration. She felt quite empty and lost as if her anchor had come loose and she didn't have anywhere to settle.

Conrad, on the other hand, seemed to be having the time of his life. Jo caught glimpses of him laughing or dancing, his blond head bent over his partner, his arm curved around her waist. He didn't seem to have any favourites among the women, and she wondered if his freewheeling style had anything to do with his role as host. He seemed determined to give everyone a good time, an attitude that she was sure motivated him to come over to her as she stood in one corner, to ask her to dance.

'No, thank you.'

'You don't dance?' He looked almost boyish with his jacket off, the tie gone and his shirt unbuttoned to reveal a tanned triangle of skin and glinting golden hair.

'I do, but . . .'

'Good, then you won't disappoint me.' He had a strong hold on her wrist and, reluctant though she was, Jo was forced to follow him into the area of the patio that had been cordoned off for dancing. He pulled her close to him, one hand firmly against the small of her back, the other clasping her hand, and skilfully rotated her in the press of couples.

They were silent for a while, and Jo tried hard not to think about the way Conrad's body was pressing against hers. It brought back memories of the night they had spent in the motel and the feel of his skin on hers, the warmth of his fingers, the sensitive, gentle motion of his mouth on . . .

Conrad's voice was cool at her ear. 'Are you satisfied with the reclamation project, New York? I haven't heard you mention mining in a week.'

Jo had brought the consultant's report home and read it, but there hadn't seemed a right time to discuss it with Conrad. 'It seems very adequate, but . . .'

'I knew it,' Conrad said, pushing her away from him

slightly and looking down at her. 'Somehow I knew you'd have an objection to something.'

Jo gave him a sweet smile that didn't quite make it to her eyes. 'There was *nothing* wrong with the report or your intentions to reclaim the orphan mines your father abandoned.'

'But . . .'

'But why don't you have a reclamation officer on the site of your present mine? You should have someone directing the men who pull debris and earth away from the blasting zones so that they'll be sloped properly for future planting of trees and . . .'

'I've been interviewing for that position for two months, New York.'

Jo looked over his shoulder at the other revolving couples. 'Oh, I see.'

'But I haven't quite found the right mixture of idealist and realist. I want someone who understands a balance sheet and corporate policy. I'm willing to spend money, but I can't afford to run Wyatt Mining into the red over reclamation.'

Jo could see his reasoning but she felt perverse. 'You do have other companies,' she pointed out, 'that are making money hand over fist.'

The grey eyes were derisive. 'Each corporate child has to make it on its own. You don't keep stealing from Peter to pay Paul.'

Jo gave him a cool smile. 'But Wyatt Mining has been stealing from nature for years. Isn't it time to replenish the earth, Conrad, for all it's given you?'

'I call that the "liberal guilt trip",' Conrad said mockingly. 'Tell me, New York, how much of your salary goes to feeding the poor, the sick and the homeless? How much of your time is devoted to taking care of the elderly? When was the last time you sent a package to starving children in India?'

'I . . .' Jo's voice trailed off in confusion as she realised that Conrad had touched upon a very vulnerable subject in her life. She had never done any of the things Conrad had suggested, and a sudden feeling of guilt came over her. During her childhood, others had fed and clothed her; others had seen to her welfare. While it was true that neither she nor Emily were still supported by the state, Jo had to concede that, in a very basic sense, they had never repaid their debt to society. People in glass houses shouldn't throw stones, she thought with a touch of irony. Her morals, in fact, were no easier to defend than Conrad's.

· While Conrad was aware that he had scored a point, he had no idea how close to home his barb had struck. 'Mouthing platitudes doesn't mean much, does it, New York?' he asked as he smoothly rotated her past a couple who were barely dancing so closely were they entwined.

'No,' she said slowly, 'it doesn't.'

He was about to speak then, but Paul was standing by them, and he tapped Conrad on the shoulder. 'Telephone, Con. Long distance.'

Conrad let go of Jo and gave Paul a questioning look. 'The Chicago office?' he asked.

'No, New York.'

'Who in New York . . .?' Conrad's voice stopped and then, with an abrupt movement, he turned on his heel and walked away.

'Dance?' Paul asked Jo who was standing very still and watching Conrad weave through the dancing couples, his blond hair turning pink, pale green and light blue under the bobbing patio lights.

'Pardon me?' she asked, suddenly realising that Paul had asked her a question.

'If you don't mind dancing with a guy with only one arm and a vast store of jokes and amusing stories to make up for the fact that he has two left feet . . .' Paul began.

'Of course, I don't mind,' Jo said with a smile. 'I have cast-iron toes.'

But as they danced, Jo found that she couldn't focus on Paul's conversation at all, her mind having followed

Conrad to the study where he had gone to take the telephone call. She was burning with curiosity to know who had called him from New York and sick with apprehension that it was Marion. She hadn't seen any letters from Manhattan for over a week and had begun to think that perhaps Emily had been right when she suggested the love affair was over. Not that there was any reason why she should give a damn about Conrad's romantic attachments; after all, she'd made it perfectly clear to him that she didn't have any intention of being another notch in his belt and she was going to return home the next day and . . .

'. . . so we'll be coming to Fairfax at Christmas,' Paul was saying.

'I'm sorry,' Jo said. 'I didn't catch that.'

'We'll come to Fairfax at Christmas to see your mother and pick up the stuff of Emily's that you can't box and send.'

'That will be nice.'

'I'd like to see Emily's part of the world,' he went on enthusiastically, 'and . . .'

Jo stopped circling with him. 'Paul, who was the call from?'

'The call?'

'For Conrad.'

Paul suddenly looked serious. 'I don't know, but I have my suspicions.'

'Suspicions?'

'It was a man's voice, but it was probably about Marion.'

'I thought that was over.'

Paul shrugged. 'It is on Con's part, but she won't give up.'

'What's she like?'

Paul pulled Jo out of the way of a couple and started dancing with her again. 'I only met her once, of course, so I didn't get to know her.'

'Well, what does she look like?' Jo asked impatiently.

'Tall, pretty, a brunette, curvaceous, sexy.'

A pang of jealousy ran straight through her like a pointed spear. 'He was in love with her?'

'I guess he was fairly well smitten for a change. He kept the Alberta phone company and mail service in business for a while, but then it sort of died off. She wanted him to move East and there was no way Conrad would do that.'

Jo could see that she wasn't going to get much information out of Paul, not because he wasn't amenable to being grilled, but because he simply didn't have the same concerns she did. There were a thousand and one things she would like to have known about Marion and Conrad's affair. How had it started? Had it gone sour only over their geographical differences? How passionate had it been? How much had Conrad loved her? But no one could answer those questions except Conrad, and Jo wasn't about to ask him. He'd made it perfectly clear that personal issues were *verboten* between them. What other man would have danced with her, held her intimately in his arms and then spent the time discussing coal reclamation?

'I think I'd like to sit this one out,' Jo said as a record changed and music with a fast beat came on. 'Do you mind?'

'Mind?' Paul asked her. 'If I look funny dancing the fox-trot, you can imagine what I'd look like doing this.'

He led her off the dance floor to the bar where, over her objections, he ordered a gin and tonic for her and proceeded to talk about Emily's plans for job-hunting. As she watched his earnest face, Jo thought how very nice Paul actually was. Now that the marriage was a *fait accompli*, she no longer had to object to him on the grounds that he was a flirt or dislike him for trying to steal Emily away from her, and Jo could appreciate his sincerity, his warmth, his pleasant good looks and his obvious love for her sister. He was, she thought, probably going to make Emily a very good husband, and even if she had apprehensions about the longevity of a marriage based on four weeks of intimacy, Jo had to acknowledge to herself that Emily and Paul had more going for them than many couples she'd known who had married after far longer engagements. They had a lot of interests in common, a similar sense of humour and they were both young enough to believe that the future held nothing but triumphs, successes and good times.

'We're going to be poor but happy,' Paul was saying when Conrad suddenly appeared at his side.

'I have to leave,' he said grimly. 'I just finished making the plane reservations.'

'You're going to New York?' Paul asked.

'To New York?' Jo echoed, and Conrad's grey eyes slid over as if she didn't even exist, as if she were merely a statue adorning his patio.

'Marion was in a car accident. It was her brother calling to tell me she's in a critical condition.'

'God, Con, I hope . . .'

But Jo interrupted, unable to hold back the words, wanting desperately to know why Conrad would fly to New York to see a woman that he was no longer tied to. 'Why?' she asked, her voice higher and shriller than she had intended, 'Why are *you* going?'

This time Conrad's glance took in the stunned look on her face, the widened amber eyes, her hands clenched together in an unconscious gesture of tension. He frowned as if her question was irrelevant, her concern inappropriate.

'Why?' he asked. 'Because she asked for me—that's why.'

CHAPTER NINE

Jo pulled her car into the parking lot before her apartment building and stared at its square bulk in the dark with the fixity of someone whose eyes can barely focus from exhaustion. She'd known it was foolish, but she'd made the trip from Calgary in three days, driving almost around the clock and only taking a quick nap at those times when her fatigue was so great, she was afraid that she'd fall asleep at the wheel. The provinces of Saskatchewan, Manitoba and Ontario had passed by her in a blur, the sameness of the prairies and then the never-ending trees, hills and lakes forming a hazy and confused memory of moving landscape. Jo couldn't remember much about her journey except for an impression of a black ribbon of road stretching ahead into infinity and the sameness of hamburgers and french fries in every truck stop across Canada.

She lugged her suitcase up the stairs to the second-floor garden apartment that she and Emily had shared and unlocked the door, standing on the threshold for a second before entering, her eyes taking in all the homely details that she had forgotten. There was the smallness of the living room with its tiny area rug, an imitation Oriental carpet of vivid blues and reds, and the huge ceramic vase that Emily had purchased on a whim to, as she put it, 'tie the whole room together'. It hadn't quite done that, but Jo could see that its deep burgundy colour did match the red of the carpet and drew the viewer's eye away from the couch which was visibly on its last legs, its dark blue corduroy torn in one corner and stretched out in another.

She leaned over and picked up a pile of mail that lay on the floor, noted that it was mostly bills and flyers and placed it on a small table. Then she dragged her heavy suitcase inside and kicked the door shut, dropping her purse as she did so and running her hands wearily through her hair, thinking how badly she needed a hot and leisurely bath to wash away the grit of travel and ease the aching of her muscles, cramped from the long hours she had spent sitting behind the wheel.

But her first inclination was to walk through the apartment, make sure that everything was in its place and connect again with parts of herself that she had left behind when she went to Calgary. She closed the door to Emily's bedroom and walked around her own, her fingers lightly touching the forest green spread on her bed, the night table where she'd left a library book and a pair of earrings in a small tray, the carved edge of her old desk, gouged and dented from the years she had used it. She opened the cream-coloured curtains even though it was night and looked out over the park that lay behind the building. Its trees were dark masses against the black sky, and the moon was narrow, a sliver of white overhead.

But for some reason Jo didn't find what she was looking for in her aimless walk around the apartment. She had yearned to be home, but her arrival didn't come up to her expectations. Being back in her apartment and mistress of all she surveyed didn't give her the lift she had anticipated. Instead she felt deflated and empty as if the rooms and pieces of furniture; bed, table and desk, no longer belonged to her. A stranger, it seemed, had once occupied this apartment: a Jo that no longer existed, a Jo who hadn't lost a sister or broken with a man who could have been her lover. The apartment which she had always thought of as tiny and cosy now appeared cramped and plain. And it wasn't the wealth of the Wyatt home that she missed or its spaciousness, Jo realised as she drifted back into the living room. It was living in a place that so beautifully reflected its surroundings—the gold and brown prairie spilling over into the earth tones of each room, the sky caught in the expanse of window and glass doors.

The phone rang shrilly as she sat down on the couch and Jo, realising who it must be, passed her hand over her eyes in a tired gesture. She didn't think that she had the energy to deal with Prudence now and break the news of Emily's marriage to her. For a moment, she debated letting it ring and then called herself both a coward and a procrastinator. What difference did it make when she told Prudence? The reaction was going to be the same whether she did it today or waited until tomorrow. Prudence was going to be dithery, upset, confused and unhappy.

'Hello?' she said, picking up the receiver.

'Jo, it's good to hear your voice!'

'Douglas,' she said flatly.

'I've been trying to reach you for days, but you haven't been in.'

'I've been away.'

'Really? Where did you go?'

Jo could just picture him, sitting beside the phone in his den, leaning back in the brown leather chair, his dark hair with its wings of silver brushed back, his long elegant fingers silently drumming the surface of his teak desk.

'I was in Calgary,' she said.

'How nice! Did you take in the Stampede?'

'Yes.'

'Delightful, isn't it?'

'I enjoyed it.'

'And Emily—did she go with you?'

'Yes.'

Douglas had a little laugh that Jo had forgotten all about, a laugh that she now heard as just a bit patronising and condescending. 'Well, you must say hello to her for me.'

'I'd like to, but she got married while we were there.'

'Little Emily married!'

'She's not so little anymore.'

'No, I guess not. Heavens, it's hard to imagine Emily as married though. How old was she when I last saw her—eighteen? And such a sweet, little thing. Well, it must have come as something of a shock to you, Jo.'

Almost, Jo thought to herself ironically, as much as this phone call. She leaned back and willed her hands to stop trembling. 'Are you phoning for any specific reason?' she asked.

This time the small laugh was uneasy. 'You always did get right to the point, Jo, didn't you?'

'I prefer it.'

Douglas cleared his throat. 'I was thinking how long it's been since we last saw one another. What was it— three years ago? A lot of water has gone under the bridge since then, and I wondered how you've been and what you've been up to.' He paused as if he hoped that she'd say something but when she didn't, he continued and Jo could hear the discomfort he was feeling in his voice, 'I've managed to get tickets to a play and, remembering how much you liked plays, I thought . . . well, I know the invitation is coming right out of the blue, Jo, but I was hoping you might accompany me to the theatre on Saturday night.'

Her first impulse was to turn him down, but something held her back—a sudden curiosity to see if her memory of him matched reality or was it a desire to test herself and see if he still had the old power over her? Jo didn't know what precisely moved her to accept Douglas' invitation, but she found herself agreeing, saying that yes, she'd be delighted to go.

'I thought you might like it.' He didn't sound awkward now, and Jo could hear the note of satisfaction in his voice. Douglas hadn't really expected her to turn him down; he believed that, after all these years and after all he had done to her, she was still in love with him. It didn't seem possible that anyone could be that arrogant, but Douglas obviously was. 'I'll pick you up at seven. The same place?'

'I haven't moved,' Jo said.

'Good. See you then.'

The telephone clicked as he hung up and Jo stared at

the phone, almost willing to believe that the conversation she had just had was a figment of her imagination. She had never thought to hear from Douglas again, not ever. In fact, she had believed for a while that he was avoiding her. They had never met at a party despite the number of people they knew in common, or crossed paths at a store or restaurant despite the smallness of the town. How odd, Jo thought as she put down the receiver, that, just at the point that she had fallen in love with another man, Douglas had come back into her life.

She had leaned her head back against the couch, but now she sat up straight and ran her hands through her hair in a sudden gesture of surprise and dismay. She spoke the words under her breath, 'Fallen in love with another man,' as if the earth would move when they were uttered aloud, but the living room was just as it had been when she entered, the smell of mustiness still in the air, the dust heavy on the end table. Had she fallen in love with Conrad? Was that what had pursued her across the continent and made her homecoming so empty of feeling? Was that the emotion which had keyed a jealousy that flayed her as if it had claws?

Conrad's departure the night of the wedding may have been merely a surprise to Paul and Emily, but it was a revelation of stunning proportions to Jo. She now understood why he had never talked about the future with her and why he had let her go so easily. With another woman in the wings, a woman who had a strong hold on his emotions, Conrad had never seen Jo as anything more than a summer flirtation, an August affair, a dalliance to pass the time while he tried to convince Marion to move to Calgary. Why else had there been so many letters? And why else had Conrad reacted so strongly to the phone call? The moment Marion had, metaphorically speaking, crooked her little finger, he had gone running.

The knowledge had hurt Jo so much that it had chased her out of the Wyatt house that night, causing her to throw her clothes into her suitcases with no regard to neatness or organisation, to pile her camping gear in a helter-skelter fashion in the back seat of the car and to leave at midnight, hastily kissing Emily and Paul goodbye and insisting that she had to go, that it would be easier to start at night, that she wasn't too tired to drive and that yes, she had to leave before the wedding celebrations were over. She had driven for more than two thousand miles as if Furies were at her back, her car eating up pavement, the hours passing by in a rush of misery.

She had thought she could run away and leave Calgary behind her, the memories so much swirling dust in the air behind her heels, but now Jo realised that nothing was that simple. Love had entered, taking a secret and circuitous journey to her heart, starting the night she had slept in a stranger's tent and reaching its destination when she lay in Conrad's embrace and told him about Douglas. She hadn't known that each meeting with Conrad, every time they had passed one another in a hallway or sat opposite one another at the breakfast table had been another step in the journey. She had read all the signals as sparks of a sexual attraction, not realising that she was falling in love gradually and that the emotion was colouring her every thought.

She had, of course, lied to herself, letting her conviction build that in leaving Calgary she would leave all her feeling for Conrad behind. The more distance she could put between them, she had thought, the more tenuous the connection. But the truth was that, underneath, Jo had never really believed that Conrad would let her go so easily. She had thought he would follow after her or, at the very least, give her some sign that their relationship would continue. Instead, he had turned his back on her, and his rejection had not only revealed the flaw in her thinking, it had also stripped off the protective barrier Jo had erected around her emotions. Love had been revealed: pure, wanting and vulnerable.

It was typical of Jo that, at this point, she stood up and looked for something physical to do. She had thought she was too tired to unpack the car and her suitcases, but the task suddenly looked inviting. She didn't want to think about what she had lost or agonise over what might have been. She didn't want to mourn the lover whose embrace she had refused. She didn't want to spend hours picking apart every conversation and meeting with Conrad until she'd accumulated a meaningless pile of phrases and words, implications and innuendoes. What Jo wanted to do was to stop thinking, to erase every emotion from her mind and to obliterate the fact that she had fallen in love with a man who most certainly didn't love her in return.

She drove to Prudence's apartment the next morning, having decided she preferred to confront her mother with the news of Emily's marriage in person rather than on the telephone. Prudence was apt to get flustered on the telephone and misunderstand what was being said. This way, she'd get the facts straight and there would be no teary, middle of the night calls like the one Jo had received several months earlier when Prudence had thought her boss was firing her because he'd talked about moving to another location in a phone message. She'd caught only the beginning of what he'd been saying and blocked out the rest in panic. It had taken Jo a couple of hours and several phone calls to figure out that The Fairfax Insurance Company wasn't moving to a new city or even just down the block—the department Prudence worked in was to be moved to another floor.

Jo pulled her car into a parking spot before a group of apartment buildings and hoped that she'd find her mother at home. It was Sunday and Prudence tended to be a late riser, often puttering around her apartment until mid-afternoon in her bathrobe with her hair still in curlers. Jo who had never been able to sleep late and was accustomed to accomplishing a full day's work before noon, tended to look down her nose at her mother's behaviour but had long ago given up trying to change her. Prudence, she recalled, had an irritating habit of agreeing with everything Jo said while merrily continuing to do her own foolish or inane thing.

It was with this last thought in her mind that Jo rang the bell to her mother's apartment and prepared herself for the coming encounter. So fixed in her mind was the image of Prudence in rollers, bathrobe and tatty, old slippers that she almost didn't recognise the woman who answered the door.

'Jo! You're home!'

She was in the door and kissing her mother's soft cheek before Jo came to terms with Prudence's appearance. She had obviously been to the hairdresser where her greying hair had been tinted a light brown and set in a flattering style around her face. Her make-up emphasised the delicate blue of her eyes and a nose that was suddenly aristocratic while drawing the viewer's eye away from the wrinkles at her mouth and the double curve of her chin. For the first time, Jo saw the reputed family resemblance between Emily and Prudence and a hint of the girlish prettiness that her mother had once possessed. Her clothes were also new; a cornflower blue pullover with matching satin trim at the neck and sleeves, a multi-coloured, floral wrap-around skirt and a pair of beige espadrilles with blue straps. The effect was sporty, stylish and quite unexpected and, for a moment, Jo only held her mother at arm's length and stared at her.

'You look wonderful,' she finally said and Prudence gave her a delighted smile.

'I've been changing my image,' she said. 'Now, come and tell me all about Calgary. Honest, Jo, you could never write a letter to save your soul and . . .' she glanced over Jo's shoulder, 'Where's Em? Didn't she come with you?'

'That's what I came . . .'

'And, Jo, wait until you see the living room. I've got

a new chair—you remember the old one with the pettipoint that was so ratty? You always hated it. Well, I gave it away and replaced it with this. Isn't it nice?'

Jo had obediently followed Prudence into the living room and was now standing before the new chair, a wing-backed chair in a dark blue plush that contrasted nicely with the lighter blue of the carpet. There were other changes as well; the shelf with the fussy knick-knacks was gone and some framed posters of events at a nearby cultural centre had been hung in its place. 'It's very nice,' Jo said.

'And you won't believe this, I'm sure. Remember Mrs Garrity who lived two houses down when we lived on Monkland Street? She died last week—simply keeled right over in the grocery store between the mayonnaise and the pickles. I tell you, Jo, when I go, I hope it's with more dignity.' Prudence shook her head and made a clucking sound with her tongue. 'Not that I have a choice, of course, but one does hope that it won't happen in such a public way.' She sat down on the couch and patted the seat beside her. 'Now, Jo, sit here and tell me all about Calgary.'

Jo sat down and gratefully took advantage of her mother's invitation. Prudence may have changed her image, but her personality was still the same. It had always been hard to keep her on to one subject; she tended to digress and go off at tangents, leading the conversation down peculiar paths and byways, her voice breathless and non-stop.

'Emily,' Jo began, 'is . . . staying in Calgary.'

'That ankle,' Prudence said. 'She really did a number on her ankle. Well, it was probably wise for her to stay rather than risk the ride home with you, and wasn't it lovely for that young man to offer you his hospitality. And it was his uncle's home, wasn't it? What were their names again?'

'Paul and Conrad. Look, I . . .'

'Not that I wouldn't do the same if two such nice young women . . . Heavens, Jo, I haven't even offered you some coffee!' She started to stand up but Jo, taking her hand, compelled her to remain seated.

'I want to tell you something.'

Prudence suddenly looked confused. 'Something bad?'

'It's about Emily. She . . . she got married while we were there.'

Her mother's soft face seemed to sag. 'Married?'

'She married Paul Wyatt just before I came home.' Prudence's lips moved as if she were trying to speak but the words wouldn't come out, and Jo felt a rush of pity. 'It was a last-minute decision and a very small wedding. We didn't think you'd be able to make it, but Paul and Emily are planning to come here at Christ . . .'

'Well, imagine that,' Prudence finally said, folding her small hands together in her lap. 'Imagine Emily married.'

The fact that Prudence had not gone to pieces took Jo by surprise. She'd anticipated everything: tears, hysterics, ranting and raving, but not this calm, this quiet. 'They're very much in love,' she said.

Prudence shook her head sadly, and Jo suddenly found that her mother was holding *her* hand and stroking it as if she were a child. 'Poor Jo,' she said. 'You've relied on Emily so much.'

Jo blinked at this reversal of the truth. 'I don't know what you mean,' she said. 'I'll be fine without Emily.'

Prudence ignored her. 'It's hard to live alone,' she said, 'and you two have been so close. I've often wondered how you would manage without Emily.'

Jo snatched her hand away. 'Don't be silly. Of course, I'll manage without . . .'

'Emily's always been the strong one,' Prudence said.

'Emily!'

'Oh, I know on the outside you're tough, Jo, but Emily's always been the one who knows exactly what she wants and goes after it. Happiness has always come easy to her. But you, Jo, well . . . you're the fighter and the person you fight hardest is yourself. I've often worried about you.'

For a moment, Jo was speechless as she absorbed the fact that Prudence was rewriting history. While it was true that Emily had always been carefree and happy, that didn't mean that Emily was strong. On the contrary, Jo had been forced to protect her for so many years—against poverty and welfare workers and difficult teachers and . . .

'Harry, there you are! I want you to meet my elder daughter, Jo, who's just come back from her holiday in Calgary.'

Jo turned to face a man who had just appeared in the curved portal of the living room; a man of about sixty-five, tall and thin with pink cheeks and blue eyes. A strong scent of cologne came with him and his thinning white hair was still damp where it had been combed along his scalp. She suddenly realised that there had been a sound in the background all during her earlier conversation with Prudence, a shower that had been running and then stopped.

'I should have written,' Prudence was saying, her cheeks suddenly flushed, 'but I thought I'd make it a surprise.'

Harry shook hands with a stunned Jo and sat down in one of the chairs, neatly pulling up the creases of his pants. He was wearing a white short-sleeved shirt and a blue tie. 'You mother loves surprises.'

'I just thought you might be upset, Jo, if I wrote you the news in a letter or phoned. I thought I'd wait until you came back to . . .'

Jo looked from one to the other. 'You're married?'

'Well, not exactly.' Prudence wavered a bit and then looked to Harry for reassurance.

He cleared his throat. 'We're living together.'

'Living together!'

'Now, Jo, everybody seems to be doing it and why . . . it wouldn't make sense for Harry and I to get married, because after I retire, it would reduce our pensions.'

'The government of the United States,' Harry said,

rolling the syllables out as if making a pronouncement, 'would rather we live in sin.'

'It isn't as if we were young, Jo. Why Harry and I are a pair of . . .'

'Old fogeys,' he finished the phrase for her and they smiled at one another.

For a second time in a month, Jo faced an alteration in the make-up of her family and the fabric of her life. She had never seen Prudence so animated or so cheerful, and it struck her that her mother had longed for another man despite the disaster that had been her marriage. And she couldn't deny that Harry's entry into Prudence's life was anything but beneficial. The house had a different air and her mother looked and acted like a different woman. The tearful and timid Prudence seemed to have disappeared completely.

'My blessings,' Jo said. 'Or is it congratulations?'

Prudence beamed at her. 'I'll bet you'll never guess where Harry and I met. I was visiting with . . .'

'Now, Pru, how about some coffee.' Harry winked at Jo. 'It's one on those long, shaggy dog stories and your mother likes to add on to it a bit to make it more distinctive. The truth is we bumped into one another at the house of a mutual . . .'

'Harry,' Prudence said reproachfully, 'it wasn't like that at all. You see, Jo, I knew Harry was going to be there because . . .'

The coffee came much later along with an assortment of Danish pastries and a platter of fruit and cheese. Jo was regaled with all the stories of Harry's courtship, Prudence's coy refusals and then ultimate surrender. It didn't seem to matter that both of them had been married before or were of an age that most of the world considered to be beyond romance. They were just as giddy and flirtatious and adoring as Emily and Paul had been.

It wasn't until Jo left them later that morning and went back to her apartment that she faced the creation of another gap in her life. Just as she had been accustomed to caring for Emily, she had gotten into the habit of looking after her mother. Fate had seemed to decree the reversal in their roles. For as long as she could remember, Jo had known that Prudence couldn't survive on her own and had taken steps to show her what to do. Her forcefulness and her determined nature had made Jo dominant in her relationship with her mother, and that dominance had bred contempt. For many years, she had regarded Prudence as silly, unmotivated, wasteful and a little bit ridiculous. But the Prudence she had seen with Harry didn't fit that mould at all. She was well-groomed, talkative without being dotty and flirtatious as a young girl.

Jo couldn't help wondering if it had been her month-long absence that had wrought such a change. Perhaps she had held Prudence under her thumb with the same control that she had wielded over Emily. Her sister had been young and forceful enough to fight for what she wanted; her mother had been forced to be devious. Jo winced at the thought as she let herself into the apartment. She hadn't liked seeing herself this way when she'd confronted Emily, and she didn't like it now. But she had to admit that she had fitted easily into the role of family arbiter, she'd grown accustomed to making decisions for other people and had considered the rest of her family as soft and weak. In fact, when she thought about it, Jo had to wonder how much of her own personality, the grit and strength in which she took so much pride, was something she had developed to prove that she was superior to Prudence and Emily. Because that's exactly how she had felt—superior.

Well, the feeling of superiority had quite evaporated. Of the three of them, Jo knew she was the most alone and the most miserable. Strength and grit may have gotten her a college education and a decent job, but on a more personal level it hadn't gotten her anything more than an empty apartment and unrequited love. Men, it seemed, preferred women who were soft and gentle, who knew how to flirt and make them feel like heroes. They didn't like women who were opinionated, argumentative and tough. Roddy's words came back to her unheeded and she envied Maria, but she suspected that he was one of a very small minority—there were very few men, she thought, who would find an independent woman sexy.

Certainly, Conrad didn't fit the category. Of course, Jo didn't know what Marion was like, but she'd received impressions of soft femininity from the delicately scented mauve stationery and that very fine script. Jo's writing paper was white and blue and her handwriting was blunt, almost square. She couldn't help feeling that she would have very little in common with Marion, and she had to acknowledge the unpalatable fact that Conrad preferred her urbane elegance to Jo's gravelly independence.

Not that she was about to change, and if her personality condemned her to a single life, then she had better learn to live with it. Jo knew she had sleepless nights ahead of her and a heart that would quicken at the sight of a blond head or dark-gold moustache. She knew that there would be days when her resolve would falter and the toughness she relied on would seem to dissolve, leaving her nothing but hurt and pain. But she also knew that she would survive; she always had before. Even as a child she had learned how to take life on the chin and keep on marching. It would take far more than a man to make Jo Davidson bite the dust.

But survival, she soon discovered, was far easier to contemplate as an abstract than as a reality. In the week that followed her meeting with Prudence, Jo learned about life without Emily. She woke up in the morning and went to bed at night to utter silence. She made meals for one and ate them standing up at the counter. The phone almost never rang, the mail was impersonal and she realised that she had never really understood just how sociable Emily had been. The only advantage of living alone was that she didn't have to fight for bathroom time in the morning, and there was always hot water for her showers, but Jo would have gladly given either up for the sight of her sister's blonde head and the sound of her cheery greeting.

She went to the community college, met with the department head, figured out her schedule, talked to a few acquaintances and then went back home. She made out a complete budget for the fall, decided that she could afford a new couch and began looking for one, a task that she hated because she'd never been the kind of person who'd enjoyed shopping. Emily would have loved picking out a new sofa, but then Emily wasn't there to do it. Jo packed up Emily's clothes into three large boxes and sent them to Calgary, thinking as she emptied the closets and drawers how often they'd fought over space to store things. Some people would have welcomed the chance to spread out and have more than enough room, but Jo would have much preferred to have her crowded closet with skirts, dresses and blouses all crammed together back just the way they had been.

She looked forward to her date with Douglas both with dread and anticipation. For one thing, it meant getting out of the apartment and talking to another human being, and she did like plays but could rarely afford to see them. On the other hand, she was nervous about seeing Douglas again and wondered what he would be like and how he would affect her. The more Jo thought about her reasons for accepting his invitation, the more she understood that the date was a test of herself. Douglas had dominated her thoughts and her actions for so long that facing him and emerging unscathed would be a triumph in itself. She knew that memories of Douglas had stopped her from making love to Conrad in the motel, and she didn't want those memories to control her anymore. Freedom Jo thought, would come from confronting her own fears.

Still, the courage to meet Douglas was something she

had to deliberately and consciously apply the way she put on the cream silk dress she'd worn at Emily's wedding and the matching high-heeled sandals. Her hair was thick, black and gleaming as it fell to her shoulders and her face was made up impeccably, bronze eye-shadow making her amber eyes tilt into the fringe of her lashes. She composed herself on the couch, leafed through a magazine that was four months old and felt that she was poised and composed until the doorbell rang, making her pulse leap and then race in panic.

Although three years had silvered his hair beyond the temples and added more lines to his face, Douglas was every bit as smooth and suave as she remembered, a tall man who prided himself on his physique and dressed in a style that could only be described as sartorial.

'Jo,' he said, walking to her and taking both her hands in his. 'You look lovely.'

'Thank you.'

He turned her slightly, tilting his head as he watched her move, an appreciative look in his brown eyes. 'The dress is new?'

She nodded, remembering the interest Douglas had taken in her clothes and the way she had dressed. At the time, she had seen it as part of his love for her, but she now realised how important appearances were to him. Douglas didn't like to go out with a woman unless she was guaranteed to turn heads as she walked.

'Very classy, Jo. Very classy.'

He was equally urbane as they walked out to the car and headed for the theatre. He talked about the university, a past trip to France, the health of his mother and the latest news of Fairfax.

'You remember Alison Ramsey who married the hotel entrepreneur?' he asked as he ushered her into the theatre and down the aisle towards their seats.

'Yes.'

'Well, he's built a magnificent place about ten miles

out of town. There's a golf course, a swimming pool, a wonderful restaurant with a great chef . . .'

He talked on and on before the curtain went up and Jo listened to him, wishing that her ears and eyes had been so clear four years earlier. There was nothing special about Douglas, not really. Granted he was a good-looking man, but he was also self-centred and egotistical. How had she managed to miss that? He barely asked her about her own doings, never mentioned her work and didn't make one reference to their past affair. As far as' Jo could see, Douglas had wiped out any memory of what had happened before and was now treating her as if she were a new date, a new woman to impress, a new and potential mirror for his vanity.

That was the word Jo would have used to describe Douglas, she thought as the curtain rose, mercifully silencing the man at her side. Vain: he was as vain as a peacock, strutting forth his wealth, his travels and his sophistication before her, spreading them out like so many iridescent feathers. She hadn't noticed his vanity four years earlier because she'd been so dazzled by his position and so eager for a father figure. Conrad had been right, she thought sadly. She had imbued Douglas with a number of qualities he hadn't had—honesty, judgment and compassion, and because she had been so blind, she'd permitted him to lead her around by the nose and make her jump through hoops of his choosing. Even stealing her research, she now understood, had been characterstic. It was quite conceivable that Douglas had never considered his article as stealing. Since she had shared her work with him, he had probably assumed her ideas were originally his.

The play was pleasant, a comedy written by a local writer that had found a mild success in an off-off Broadway production, but when Douglas suggested that they go for dessert afterwards, Jo begged off, saying that she had a slight headache. So he drove her home, expounding on the play they had seen, plays he had seen before and the plays he wanted to see when he visited Manhattan later that month. When he pulled up before her apartment, he turned off the ignition and leaned towards her, his arm resting behind her shoulders.

'I could find my way to this place with my eyes shut,' he said.

So he did remember. 'You did come often,' Jo said warily.

'It's too bad we had to break it off that way.'

We? 'I don't really think . . .'

'I've missed you, Jo. I found that you're in my thoughts a lot, and I admit to a bit of nostalgia for what we had. All those wonderful conversations and . . .' his voice dropped into a more sensual note, 'those marvellous hours in bed. It was good, wasn't it, Jo?'

If there was ever a chance for Jo to take her revenge, it was now. His arm had tightened around her shoulders and his expression spoke louder than his words. Douglas had spent the week anticipating another affair, his ego inflating to the point that she could burst it with one swift and lethal jab. And she had so much ammunition; she could question his professional competence and cut his sexual pride to shreds. For the first time since he had left her, Jo felt that she held Douglas in the palm of her hands. One word, a simple *no*, one squeeze and he would be . . .

But Jo didn't take advantage of the opportunity he was offering to her and say what she had dreamed of saying for so many years, and it wasn't because she didn't enjoy revenge. What Jo had suddenly discovered was that she simply didn't care and that, in fact, she felt pity for Douglas, wondering how many women he needed to bolster an ego so shallow and so fragile that it required constant feeding. He was nothing without his mirrors, the women he chose to reflect himself, and Jo realised that there wasn't anything she could say to him that would stop him or change his behaviour. If she hurt him badly enough, he would turn faster to the next woman in a frantic attempt to obliterate her words with another woman's adoration. And he'd find her, of course. There were plenty of women who had been as naïve and vulnerable as Jo.

So she simply opened the car door and slipped out from under his arm, saying as she did so, 'Thanks for the evening.'

A puzzled look came across his face. 'Well, I'll call you, Jo. There's another play . . .'

Jo stood beside the car, holding the door open. 'I'm sorry, Douglas, but I really can't commit myself to anything right now.'

His look of bewilderment was replaced by cunning, and he leaned over further so he could see her face in the dim light of the street lamps. 'Jo,' he said in a soothing tone, 'I'm easy. It's just that I think we have such rapport that it would be . . .'

Jo didn't think she could stand any more of Douglas's 'fancy jargon' as Conrad would have put it. 'Good night,' she said, closing the door in his face and taking a small satisfaction in his sharp, surprised movement backwards to the wheel.

She hoisted her purse to her shoulder and walked towards her apartment building with a sensation of weightlessness so strong that Jo could have sworn that she was stepping on air. She had never known how ponderous her memories had been. She had never realised the extent to which her affair with Douglas had burdened her. Everything she had said and done had been marked with the stain of her failure. But now she was free of him; indifference and pity replacing her guilt, her anger and, yes, she could admit it now, a yearning that he would take her back.

Jo smiled into the starry night, the feeling of triumph dazzling and bright. It was true that she had no other man to turn to, and that the man she would have chosen didn't want her, but Conrad's rejection couldn't diminish her newly found buoyancy and exhilaration. She had won a personal battle in which the prize was her own highly valued sense of integrity and independence. And it had been so easy, so ridiculously easy that she wanted to laugh out loud and fling her arms wide to embrace the world. She was free, free, free . . .

CHAPTER TEN

WHEN she got into her apartment, Jo stripped off her clothes and put on a robe, thinking that she would make herself a drink to celebrate her newly found liberation. She wished that Emily could have been there to share the moment with her; she would understand the depths of Jo's satisfaction and the courage it had taken to achieve it. But, of course, Emily wasn't there; she was back in Calgary playing house with Paul—at least that's the way Jo thought of it. Despite the fact that her sister was over twenty-one, Jo still found it hard to think of her as married in the true sense of the word. Wishing for Emily was futile, of course, so she shrugged and went into the narrow kitchen with its old-fashioned gas range and tiny refrigerator where she mixed herself a gin and tonic, her bare feet cold on the linoleum.

She was just slicing a lime when the doorbell rang and, for a second, she hesitated. Douglas had come back; she had suspected he might, knowing that he'd find her rejection unbelievable and that his bruised ego would require solace. He would want to change her mind, talk her into another affair and convince her that there wasn't anyone else in the world who could make her as happy as he could. Jo put down the lime and walked to the door, ready to battle him once again, her confidence so high and so sure that she knew she could get rid of him in five minutes flat.

But it wasn't Douglas standing in the doorway in his elegant charcoal suit, his silvered hair gleaming in the light, it was Conrad wearing a cream-coloured stetson, a denim jacket over a pale blue shirt, jeans and a pair of brown boots. He stepped across the threshold as she stood there motionless, utterly unable to speak. H

170

closed the door behind him, walked into the centre of the living room, glanced around at the furniture and then turned to look at her.

'Who was that?' he asked and beneath the shadow cast by the brim of his hat, Jo could see the strained lines that ran from his mouth to his nose and the fact that his jaw was clenched.

'Who?'

'The guy in the car.'

'Oh, that was Douglas.'

He took off the stetson then and, holding it in his fingers, rubbed his forehead with the back of his hand, before dropping his arm to his side. His hair held the impression of his hat in dark-gold ridges at his temples. 'You're going out with Douglas again?' he asked.

Jo shook her head. 'Exorcising a ghost.'

He slipped a hand into the pocket of his jeans. 'Did it work?'

'Yes.' There was a pause. 'And Marion? How is she?'

'She's okay. She's out of the hospital and back home.'

'That's . . . good.'

'I was doing the same—exorcising part of my past.' Her voice was surprisingly steady. 'Did it work?'

'Yes.'

They looked at one another for a long time then, and the rhythm of Jo's heart, which had raced at the sight of Conrad at her door, steadied to a pace far more satisfying, far more fulfilling. She wanted to reach out and touch the lines of fatigue on his face; she wanted to run her fingers once again through the thick waves of his hair; she wanted to . . .

'That's quite a confection you're wearing,' he said.

'Confection? Oh,' she glanced down at herself, 'you mean my robe.' It had been a gift from Douglas and she hadn't worn it in years, but she had put it on tonight without a thought of its origins. It was an ivory robe of satin with see-through ecru lace at the yoke and full, flowing sleeves. It covered her from neck to toes, but it clung to her curves and the colour set off the darkness of her complexion, the amber of her eyes and the black gleam of her hair.

'You mind if I ask you a personal question?'

She glanced back up at him warily. 'No.'

'Are you wearing anything underneath it?'

Jo couldn't stop her lips from curving upwards. 'No,' she said.

With one movement of his arm, Conrad set his stetson spinning in the air, its cream-coloured rim making rapid circles before it landed flat on the sofa.

She was looking at it when he said, 'I'm going to make love to you, New York. I've waited long enough.'

'And how long is that?' she asked softly.

'Thirty-nine days, fourteen hours, twenty-six minutes and nineteen seconds.' And when she smiled, he added, 'The last is for the time I sat out in the car and waited for you to come home.'

They were still standing yards apart, but Jo could feel heat rise wherever his grey glance fell, on the curve of a hip under the ivory satin, the outline of a breast, the soft curve of her mouth. Her skin felt so sensitive suddenly that the robe seemed oppressive, hot and heavy. She lifted her hands to the neck of it and began unbuttoning the small satin buttons that ran to her toes, her fingers trembling slightly as she worked them through the tiny buttonholes. He watched with narrowed eyes as her throat was revealed where it joined the hollow between her shoulderblades, then the swelling tops of her breasts with their delicate tracing of veins. As her hands moved lower, one edge of the robe fell to the side, baring a breast, its nipple dark-rose and pointed, its roundness shadowing the cleft where her fingers worked.

Conrad was beside her then, scooping his arm under her knees and picking her up to carry her into the bedroom. They said nothing as he let her down on the bed and then took off his own clothes, the sound of his boots thudding to the floor, his buckle unclasping, the pearly white studs on his shirt unsnapping in rapid succession as he threw off his jacket and shirt. And still they said nothing as he kneeled down beside her and his large fingers leisurely finished the job she had begun.

The light from the living room illuminated the bedroom so faintly that she couldn't see anything but the outline of his body, and she tentatively touched his shoulder and then cupped it with her hand, feeling the sleekness of his skin and the way his muscles moved as he worked the final button at her ankles. He slid down beside her so that his shoulder was close to her ear and he lazily traced a line that began at her forehead, went over her nose, outlined her mouth and then moved to her throat. Jo swallowed as his fingers moved lower, circling the fullness of one breast as it fell slightly to the right of her rib cage, dipping into the indentation of her belly button, grazing her hip bone, and then with slightly more pressure, sliding into the intimate curve of her.

'You're ready,' he said.

'Yes.' She had been ready at almost the moment she had seen him in her doorway, his stetson shading his eyes. She had felt the tightening deep within her, that precursor of desire, the signal that sent a sensuous warmth flooding into every vein.

He took his hand away, and she couldn't prevent a small moan from escaping her lips. 'Oh, Jo,' he said, pulling her into his arms so that they lay face-to-face, and she could feel the whole length of him against her, their chests meeting, the heat and hardness of his arousal against her stomach, their knees touching. 'It's taken so long.'

She turned her head and glanced at the digital clock with illuminated numbers. 'Not so long,' she said. 'Ten minutes to be exact—since you knocked on the door.'

She could hear the laughter in his voice. 'So you do have a sense of humour.'

'It's taken a long time for me to develop one.'

'I'll never forget the night you come back from the Stampede. I was so damned jealous.'

'Of Roddy?'

'No, I knew Roddy was engaged and I had my suspicions as to why he'd taken you out. It was that you looked so different from the Jo I knew. For a second I didn't recognise you.'

'It was the silly hat and souvenirs.'

'No, it was the expression on your face. I could tell that you'd been laughing and I envied Roddy's ability to make you so happy.'

'I spent the whole time wishing Roddy were you.' Jo stroked his back, feeling the small bones of his spine, the width of muscle. It was her turn to trace the planes and angles of his body, to feel its masculinity beneath her fingers and to know that he wanted her.

'Watch it,' he said, his breath catching as her fingers tangled in the golden hair at his belly. 'I'm not answerable for the consequences.'

'Conrad . . .?'

'Mmmm.'

'I'm not on the pill or anything.'

His hand brushed her cheek. 'I'll take care of it,' he said.

'And . . . and I haven't been with a man in a long time . . .'

'It's like riding a bicycle, New York. You never forget.'

'Promise?'

'Promise, darling.'

And he was as good as his word. Their lovemaking was like a dance, a coming together and moving apart and then back again, the silky touch of skin against skin, a warmth that gathered slowly into a hot, racing intensity. Their mouths met, tongues mingling; his hands pulled her so close that she could feel the pounding of his heart against her breasts. She did everything she had wanted to do in the past: explored the shape of his face, caressing the curve of his eyes, feeling the length of his lashes, the boniness of his nose, the silken bristle of his moustache. She came to know the way his skin stretched over the muscles of his chest, the indentations between his ribs, the concavity below where his abdomen yielded to his groin. His legs were long like hers, but not as smooth. Muscles knotted under the fine brush of hair; even his buttocks were hard. The only softness that Jo could find was at the back of his knee.

'That tickles, New York,' he growled.

'There—is this better?'

His hand brushed the top of her head. 'I thought you said you hadn't made love in a long time.'

'I'm just practising.'

'Practising for what?'

'The real thing.'

She felt him tug at her hair, pulling her up towards him. 'Is that what you're waiting for?'

And the real thing was better than Jo had ever known it could be. Douglas had touched her with competence; Conrad touched her with love, and she responded with sensations she had never felt before. She trembled when he entered her, and when he gathered her closer, his hands on her thighs, she felt him touch deep within her. From there, the pulsing of desire spread like ripples on a lake, moving outwards, filling every part of her, reaching, reaching . . . until she shook with the force of her own body and cried out his name, her fingers gripping him so hard that later they would find her mark on him, each shoulder bearing an arc of tiny bruises and small curved welts.

They lay together for a long time entwined, their legs tangled together, their bodies still joined. Jo's cheek rested against Conrad's neck and she could feel the pulse that beat there. Her hair was damp and the cooling perspiration on her skin made her shiver a bit.

'Getting cold?' he asked softly.

'A bit.'

They untangled then, climbed under the covers and curled up together, Conrad's hand resting idly on one breast, the other slowly caressing her hip. 'Tell me about Douglas,' he said.

Jo snuggled closer against him. 'He called up and asked me out. I went because I had to find out why I had let him dominate me the way he had. He isn't even nice, Conrad, that's what I discovered. The Douglas I knew was a figment of my imagination not a reality.'

'So his shadow won't follow you around any more?'

She shook her head. 'And I learned why I couldn't make love to you that night in the motel.'

'Why?'

'Because I linked his dominance over me with sex. I couldn't separate the two, and I thought that making love would make me subservient and submissive to you—the way I was with Douglas.'

'I can't imagine you as submissive.'

'No, honourable master?' she asked, teasingly.

He poked her slightly. 'No, and I wouldn't want you to be. Hell, Jo, I don't want a slave; I want a woman with a mind of her own. I like ornery women; they make life interesting.'

'Was . . . Marion ornery?'

'I had a feeling I was going to have to confess about Marion.'

Jo turned over so that they were lying face-to-face. 'I want to know about every woman you ever slept with.'

'It would be a hell of a boring list, New York. A series of one night stands and casual encounters. I can't even remember some of them.'

'Marion didn't sound like a casual encounter.'

'She was different; she was . . . the truth is I'd never met anyone quite like her before. She was as liberated as they come, knew her own mind and was sophisticated to her fingernails. She intrigued me and I got involved, but when I really began to understand what made her tick, I knew the affair wouldn't last. Marion thrived on the city—the excitement, the fast pace, the name-dropping, the cocktail parties. Jo, the first time I stayed with her in New York, she dragged me to so many cocktail parties where I had to make polite conversation while trying to balance a drink in one hand a bait on a cracker in the other, that I thought I'd pass out from boredom and starvation.'

'Did you tell her?'

'I did. We fought like hell over my wants versus hers, and I knew it wasn't going to work. They say opposites attract, but we couldn't have stayed together for a week. And it didn't take me long to figure out that I was a novelty for her, a token cowboy to take to cocktail parties. She enjoyed putting me on display, but when she came to Calgary, I could see that she thought my friends were country bumpkins.'

'But she still wrote to you, Conrad, and when she had the accident . . .'

He shifted restlessly against her. 'She couldn't believe me when I told her that there wasn't a chance of my even considering a move East, so she'd write and telephone, cajole and beg. And then when her brother phoned, telling me she'd crashed the car and he thought she was on drugs because she had been so depressed over me . . . well, what could I do? I had to go and see her. I had to talk to her and tell her that it was over.'

'How do you know she'll believe you this time?'

'I told her I'd fallen in love with another woman.'

Jo didn't think she'd ever heard words so beautiful. 'And have you?' she whispered.

'No,' he said mockingly. 'I travelled all the way back to Calgary, turned around, got on a plane three hours later, flew all the way back, rented a car in Syracuse, spent three hours on the road and then sat in your parking lot for twenty-six minutes and nineteen seconds because I don't love you.'

'You went all the way back to Calgary?'

'I've crisscrossed this continent so many times in the last week Air Canada is going to put me on permanent standby.'

'What made you come back?'

'A mixture of sisterly persuasion, brotherly encouragement and the feeling that if I didn't come after you now, I'd lose you.'

Jo kissed him gently on the cheek. 'I thought you didn't care if I left.'

'I didn't know how to stop you.' Conrad gave a helpless shrug as if the memory was still sharp. 'I tried every way I knew how to hook you, New York. The blunt, direct routes scared you so much that I tried companionable intimacy and when that didn't work, I couldn't figure out what to do. I didn't have a room full of etchings, and I'm not the kind of guy who goes in for sweet talk. You were the most stubborn, ornery, exasperating female I'd ever come across.'

'Keep the compliments coming. I love them.'

'And touchy.'

'Oh, Conrad,' she said sweetly. 'Why did you put up with me?'

'Because I fell for you like a ton of bricks. When I saw you in the hospital, I thought you were one of the sexiest women I'd ever seen. And then when you gave me that song and dance about the head of Wyatt Mining being a ruthless plunderer, I knew I had to have you. I wish you could have seen your face that night with the firelight flickering over your earnest, angry frown. I knew I was going to have more fun with you than anyone I'd ever met.'

'And has it been . . . fun?'

Conrad groaned and tightened his arms around her. 'It's been torture; you led me around in circles. I never knew what the hell you'd pull next.'

'Good,' she said with satisfaction. 'Now, we're even.'

'They don't make 'em meaner than you, do they, New York?'

'Uh-uh.' And she kissed him just to emphasise the point.

'Anyway, when I got back to Calgary, Paul and Emily insisted that I go after you. They were positive that you were madly in love with me because you left the night of the wedding in such a state of misery. Your sister had me turned around, ticketed, stamped and ready to fly before I knew it. When Emily decides that she wants something, she gets it.'

Jo was silent for a minute and then spoke, her voice reflective, 'My mother said something to me about Emily that I thought was crazy, but the more I think about it . . .'

'About what?'

'She said that, of the two of us, Emily was the stronger because she knew what she wanted and she aimed for happiness whereas I was always fighting someone, usually myself.'

'I always thought your relationship with Emily was peculiar, Jo. I tried to tell you that.'

'I think . . . well, I think now that Emily let me control her because it made life easier for her. Certainly, when my wishes went against hers over Paul, she rose up in rebellion. And I . . . I used Emily as protection against the world. I didn't have to interact with anyone else because I had her. I didn't realise it at the time, of course. I thought I was shielding her from the harsh realities of life but, in fact, it was quite the opposite. Her presence allowed me to believe that I didn't need a man or a family or even friends, and by focusing on her, I didn't have to dwell on my own problems.'

'She loves you,' he said gently. 'She's very proud of you.'

'Oh, Conrad,' she said twining her arms around his neck. 'I've made a mess of things, haven't I?'

'Yup.'

'But they're better now?'

'Mmmm.'

'Not again!'

'Why not, New York? You've got something against sex?'

'Not with you,' she whispered. 'Not with you.'

When Jo awoke it was near eleven o'clock in the morning, and Conrad was still sleeping, his blond hair tousled on the pillow, his shoulder bare and tanned above the white hem of the sheet. She thought about all the travelling he had done and, deciding to let him sleep, carefully moved his arm from around her waist and slipped out of the bed. He mumbled something and then turned over, once again in a deep sleep.

Jo showered, humming to herself and smiling occasionally as she thought about the night before, pulled on a pair of jeans and a blue velour top and went to a nearby corner store for the newspaper and food for breakfast. Since she'd been living alone, she'd given up eating anything before noon, but she remembered the way Conrad and Paul could consume Mrs Beattie's pancakes and thought she'd better stock up. Conrad was still asleep when she got back so she made herself a cup of coffee, sat down on the couch, grimaced as another spring popped out of the torn upholstery and started to go through the paper.

The telephone rang as she was reading and she picked up the receiver and heard Emily's voice.

'Is he there?'

Jo couldn't resist keeping the suspense going just a little bit longer.

'Who?' she asked innocently.

'Conrad—he was supposed to be there by now.' Emily sounded worried. 'I gave him good directions.'

'Oh, yes, he made it.'

'And?'

'And what?'

'Come on, Jo. What happened?'

'Well, he got here and rang the doorbell. I let him in . . .'

'Jo!' Emily's voice was almost a shriek.

'All right,' Joe said in the same deadpan voice. 'We made mad, passionate love all night.'

Pause. 'Is that the truth?'

'Yup.'

'How many times?'

'Em! What a nosy thing to ask!'

Jo could hear Emily's muffled laughter. 'Now I know you did.'

'Married life has made you sneaky.'

'Oh, Jo, you won't guess what married life has actually done.'

'What?'

'It's gotten me pregnant.'

Jo's newpaper hit the floor with a thud. 'You're joking.'

'Isn't it wonderful!'

'I thought you said that Paul knew how to . . .'

Emily giggled. 'I must be like Mrs Beaulieu—remember her? She used to get pregnant whenever her husband threw his pants over the end of the bed.'

'A baby is a serious business, Em. A baby is a responsibility.'

'We know that.'

'I don't think you do. You have no money, Paul is still in school, you don't have a job, your apartment is going to be too small . . .'

'I have a family, Jo,' Emily said, her voice intense and strong. 'And that's what's really important.'

What could Jo say? She knew exactly how Emily felt; she knew what it was like to yearn for a father and to wish for a normal family. Both she and Emily had wanted a father who worked and a mother who stayed home. They had wanted home-baked cookies in the cookie jar, family picnics and a father who wore slippers at night while he read the newspaper before a roaring fire. It hadn't mattered that their image was cliché-ridden or totally unrealistic—that was how families were portrayed in their readers at school and that's what they longed for—that warm and lovely sense of stability that comes from a house that is filled with love.

So in a way, Jo couldn't blame Emily and Paul for being thrilled at the prospect of a baby. The infant would make them more than just newly-weds; it would make them a family unit—a father, a mother and a child. The thought of the same thing happening to Conrad and herself made a suspicious dampness come to her eyes. Jo cleared her throat. 'It sounds wonderful, Em,' she said softly. 'I'm happy for you.'

'When are you coming back?'

'I don't know.'

'Hasn't Conrad *said* anything?'

'We . . . didn't spend much time talking.'

Emily laughed. 'Ask him to marry you, Jo, and get the suspense over with.'

'I can't ask Conrad to marry me,' Jo protested.

'Why not?'

'Emily, did you ask Paul to marry you?' Jo asked suspiciously.

'Of course I did,' Emily said in a gay voice. 'I couldn't sit around and wait for him to pop the question. Now, listen, Jo, you've always told me how women are equal to men. Prove it; propose to Conrad.'

'I'm hanging up on you,' Jo threatened.

'Coward.'

'Goodbye, Emily,' Jo said firmly.

'I dare you, Jo. I dare you to do it.'

'Give my love to Paul.'

Emily's last words were a childhood taunt. 'Scaredy-cat.'

Marriage. Jo hadn't given any thought to the future the night before; it had seemed far more important to understand and explain the past. She and Conrad hadn't talked about anything beyond the pleasure of the moment, and she had no idea how he envisioned their relationship. Oh, she was fairly certain that a marriage was on the cards, and she wasn't too concerned about legalising their enjoyment of one another, but she hadn't given a thought to her career and what a move to Calgary would mean.

Would she be able to teach when she got there? She could never get a job in a university because she hadn't gotten a doctorate, and she had no idea whether there was a community college in Calgary. She wasn't the kind of geologist who could work for oil companies; she hadn't been trained in the study of land formations in which oil developed. She couldn't even be the reclamation officer in Conrad's mine. For one thing, she was admittedly too idealistic and for another, she didn't want to live in Crow's Nest Pass while Conrad lived in Calgary. She didn't think absentee marriages worked very well.

The more she mulled over the problem, the more upset Jo became. She knew that she wouldn't be happy unless she was working. She knew that Conrad's love for her and her love for him wouldn't be enough if she was stuck in a house with nothing more to do than watch Mrs Beattie clean. And Jo was introspective enough to know that, while she would love having children, she couldn't be a full-time mother. Her whole identity was bound up with what she was professionally; she'd fought far too hard to reach her present position to want to give it up.

Jo dropped the newspaper and stared despondently at the floor, her unhappiness so profound that she felt as if the words and embraces she and Conrad had exchanged the night before had never existed. She couldn't give up her profession for love and she didn't want to give up her lover for a job. The dilemma was so painful that Jo forgot about Conrad's need for sleep. She walked into the bedroom, climbed up on the bed and shook him by the shoulder.

'It's almost one o'clock,' she said, 'and . . . and it isn't going to work.'

One grey eye opened and then shut again. For a moment, Jo thought that Conrad had gone back to sleep, but he rolled over on to his back and groaned, throwing his forearm across his eyes as the sun touched his face.

'Conrad,' she continued, her voice upset and urgent, 'I've thought it over and I . . .' she swallowed painfully, feeling the lump come to her throat, 'I can't marry you.'

'One o'clock?' he mumbled. 'It's that late?'

'But we could see each other on holidays.' She'd just thought of that. 'And vacations. I'm a wonderful letter writer and we could phone and . . .'

'Who was that on the phone?'

Jo wondered if Conrad had gone selectively deaf. 'Emily. She's pregnant.'

He put his arm down and stared at her. 'Pregnant?'

'As in b-a-b-y.'

'Those crazy kids.'

'That's what I told her. They haven't two nickels to rub together and Paul still has two years of school and Em doesn't have a job.'

Conrad stretched and yawned. 'We'll manage. I've got enough money and Mona will probably cough up something although she'll hate admitting that she's a grandmother.' He pulled himself up, not caring that the sheet fell away from his body, making Jo's heart beat just a little bit faster, and added with a growl, 'How about something to eat? I'm starving. After all, I put in at least two hours of exercise last night.'

Jo couldn't help blushing. 'You didn't hear what I said.'

'Sure I did. You said that we couldn't get married.'

She clenched her hands together. 'I don't think I could get a job in Calgary and I'm not the type to stay home—I'd make you absolutely miserable if I was bored and had time on my hands and . . .'

'Really.'

She drew herself up. 'My career is just as important to me,' she said with dignity, 'as yours is to you.'

'And?'

'And I wouldn't be able to teach; I couldn't work at your mine on reclamation because it would mean living in Crow's Nest; I'm not an oil geologist; I . . .'

'Oh,' said Conrad, reaching for her and pulling her into his arms, 'is that all?'

'All?' she echoed. 'Don't you see what it means?'

'I called Roddy during my short stay in Calgary

between flights to and from New York.' Conrad interrupted his words to kiss her on the neck below her ear and then said, 'I haven't shaved. Do you mind?'

Jo ignored his last statement and twisted around to face him. 'Roddy?'

'Well, if you don't mind.' He nuzzled her neck and made pleasurable sounds. 'You've got the nicest neck, New York—in addition to great legs and absolutely sensational breasts. Have I told you that yet?'

The compliments were almost enough to distract her, and Jo couldn't help smiling. 'No, but flattery isn't going to get you anywhere.'

'You'd rather talk about Roddy?' he asked in mock-despair.

'Yes,' she said firmly.

'He needs a partner for his consulting company.'

'Oh,' Jo breathed.

'And it's yours if you want it.'

The weight of her worries fell off her instantaneously. 'I'd love it.'

'Mmmm—that's what I figured.'

She snuggled closer to him, not at all minding that the face was bristly with golden hair. The nude length of him was stretched out before her, and she was thinking how lovely it was going to be to wake up every morning with that body beside her, knowing that it was hers for the asking. She contemplated with utter contentment the thought of a daily life with Conrad, the both of them working in similar fields, the conversation of two like minds, the perfect match of their personalities. Marriage with Conrad was going to be wonderful except that . . .

'What about a contract?' she asked.

This time she had taken him by surprise. 'A contract?' he asked, lifting his head from her shoulder where he had been placing a string of soft kisses. 'What sort of a contract?'

'A marriage contract. Roddy and Maria have one.'

'You mean how we divide up the property and who

gets to supervise Mrs Beattie and which parent assumes the burden of dirty diapers if we have kids?'

Jo nodded. 'It isn't a bad idea.'

'There's one drawback,' he said.

'What's that?'

'I haven't asked you to marry me.'

'Conrad!'

He grinned lazily. 'Of course, I've been considering the possibility. You are, after all, a fairly attractive woman; I hear tell that you can boil water and . . .'

'You like teasing me, don't you?'

'I love it, New York. And I love you.'

'I love you, too,' she whispered.

He ruffled her hair. 'I suspected it for a long time, but I knew you were too stubborn to say so.'

'I fell in love with you the night we slept together in your tent.'

'Who do I thank for holes in tents and mountain storms?'

She smiled. 'And you'd better add sleeping bags for one.'

'And you, Jo,' he said pulling her into his arms. 'I will always give thanks for you.'

BARBARA DELINSKY
Fingerprints

Carly Quinn is a
woman with a past.
Born Robyn Hart, she
was forced to don a new
identity when her intensive
investigation of an arson-ring
resulted in a photographer's death
and threats against her life.

Ryan Cornell's entrance into her life
was a gradual one. The handsome
lawyer's interest was piqued, and then
captivated, by the mysterious Carly — a
woman of soaring passions and a
secret past.

FP-2